I0663014

THE GUNSMITH

450

The Ambush of Belle Starr

Books by J.R. Roberts
(Robert J. Randisi)

The Gunsmith series

Lady Gunsmith series

Angel Eyes series

Tracker series

Mountain Jack Pike series

COMING SOON!

The Gunsmith
451– The Last Way West

For more information visit:
www.SpeakingVolumes.us

THE GUNSMITH

450

The Ambush of Belle Starr

J.R. Roberts

SPEAKING VOLUMES, LLC
NAPLES, FLORIDA
2019

The Ambush of Belle Starr

ISBN 978-1-64540-103-2

Chapter One

Clint Adams had one, and only one, protégé—Roxy Doyle, also known as Lady Gunsmith. He met her when she was young and searching for her father. She had a gun, and the courage to use it, but only her natural skill. He took that skill and honed it, turned it into something that would serve her well and keep her alive until she accomplished her quest.

That was some years ago, and since then he had seen her only once. But he heard of her exploits, and knew that she still searched for her father, Gavin Doyle, the bounty hunter. That was why she had sent him a telegram in Labyrinth, Texas, asking him to do her a favor.

Many times over the years, people had asked him for favors, and they usually led to him either killing or almost being killed. Of late he had begun to grant fewer and fewer of them, but a request from Lady Gunsmith could not be ignored . . .

***

He was in his hotel room in Labyrinth, enjoying the company of Sonya, one of the girls who worked in Rick's Place, his friend Rick Hartman's saloon.

Sonya was a dark-haired beauty whose eye fell on Clint as soon as he entered.

"Who's that?" he had asked Rick.

"New girl," Rick said. "Hired her since you were here last."

They went to Rick's table, where the bartender brought them two beers.

"He's new, too," Clint said.

"Yes," Rick said, "meet Tim Kitchen. Tim, this is Clint Adams."

Kitchen, a tall, beefy man of the type Rick liked to keep behind his bar to serve drinks as well as keep the peace, stuck his hand out and said, "Glad to meetcha."

Clint shook the man's hand, and the barman returned to work.

"Big fella," Clint said.

"And damned good at his job," Rick said. "How long do we have you for this time, Clint?"

"I can't say," Clint said. "I'm kind of tired and want to give Eclipse some time off. He's not getting any younger."

"You might be ready for a new horse, then."

Clint sipped his beer and didn't comment. Instead, he watched the new girl, Sonya, as she walked around the room. She moved with grace and stood with poise that should have been on a stage, not on a saloon floor.

"Are you listening to me?" Rick asked.

"No, I'm not," Clint said, "I'm watching this girl work your floor. She doesn't belong here. She doesn't belong in a saloon."

"I know that," he said, "you know that, but she doesn't seem to know that."

"And she's not a kid," Clint said. "How old is she? Twenty-six?"

"Twenty-eight. She got off the stagecoach, came in here and asked me for a job. I'm no fool. I gave her one."

"Bring her over so I can meet her."

"Wow," Rick said, "I thought you'd ask me to do that when you first walked in."

Rick introduced them, and they took an immediate liking to each other. And Clint believed she liked him, not the Gunsmith, but Clint Adams, the man.

"Have a drink?" Clint asked her.

She looked at Rick.

"Go ahead," he said, standing up. "I have work to do."

Rick held his chair for her, then walked away after she sat.

"Champagne?" Clint asked.

"How did you know?"

"You look like a woman with expensive tastes."

Clint turned and looked at Tim Kitchen, who simply nodded and came over with a glass of champagne and two glasses.

"Just for the lady," Clint said. "I'll stick to beer."

"Right," Kitchen said.

He poured a glass for Sonya.

"Thanks, Kitch."

"Should I leave the bottle?"

"I don't think so," she said. "I want to keep my head around Mr. Adams."

"Yes, Ma'am."

Kitchen returned to the bar.

Clint and Sonya talked, got acquainted, then said what they were both thinking.

"We should get even better acquainted," she said.

"Just what I was thinking."

"Your hotel room, when I'm done here?"

"I'll be waiting."

He got up to leave, put his hand out and took the champagne bottle from Kitchen on the way out.

Chapter Two

They got better acquainted in his room, over champagne, for three nights straight. On the fourth morning he woke, rolled over, and stared at her bare back as she lay, naked, on her stomach. The line down the center of her back to her butt cheeks was the most graceful he had ever seen.

He leaned over and followed the curve of her spine with his tongue. When he reached the cleft between her ass cheeks he lingered. She moaned and awoke, then laughed.

"How low do you intend to go?" she asked.

"As low as it took to wake you," he said.

"Mmm," she said, spreading her legs, "I don't think I'm quite awake."

He laughed this time, rolled her over onto her back, and then nestled down between her legs. He pressed his face to the very dark, bushy patch between her legs, probed with his tongue until she groaned. As she grew wetter, he lapped it up. By the time his cock was fully hard. He raised himself above her and drove into her.

"Oh, yes," she said, wrapping her legs around his waist, "now this is the way to wake up . . ."

***

They were lying entwined together when the knock came at his door.

"Rick?" she asked.

"No," Clint said, "He knows better."

Clint got up from the bed, padded naked to the door with his gun in his hand.

"Who is it?"

"Telegram Mr. Adams," a male voice said.

"Slide it under the door."

"Yes, sir."

Clint looked, saw the yellow slip of paper come sliding in.

"Thank you," he said. "I'll come by later with a tip."

"Yes, sir."

He heard the footsteps go off down the hall, then bent to pick up the telegram. He carried it back to the bed, holstered the gun before reading it.

"Trouble?" she asked, touching his back.

"I don't know."

"In my experience, telegrams are never good news," she said. "Do you want me to leave before you read it?" she asked. "I have to go, anyway."

"Maybe that'd be best," he said. "Thanks."

She leaned over, kissed his shoulder, then rose off the bed and got dressed. One more kiss and she headed for the door, but stopped.

"How many of Rick's girls have you brought up here over the years?" she asked.

"A few," he admitted.

She smiled.

"I just wanted to see if you'd lie and tell me I was the first."

"I don't lie," he said.

"I know that now," she said. "See you later?"

"I'll come by the saloon," he promised.

She nodded and left.

He looked at the telegram in his hand. He agreed with Sonya to a point. Telegrams often brought bad news. But then, you never knew until you read them.

He unfolded it and saw that it was from Roxy Doyle. She needed him to go to Oklahoma Territory and help Belle Starr. She wasn't able to do it, because she thought she was close to finding her dad. He folded the telegram again. She always felt she was close to finding her father, but hadn't yet. He wondered if she ever would.

He remembered Roxy had met and made friends with Belle Starr some time ago. So it was no surprise that Belle would reach out to her. He wondered how the outlaw queen would feel when he showed up.

Well, with that thought, he figured he had already decided he was going to the Oklahoma Territory to help Belle Starr . . .

***

When Clint left his hotel, he went directly to the telegraph office to send a reply to Roxy. It was brief. It said: ON MY WAY. He paid the clerk, and tipped him, as well.

Then he went to Rick's Place, which was closed, but he knew he could get breakfast there.

It was Kitchen who opened the door and let him in. He joined Rick at his table, and Kitchen brought out some ham-and-eggs and coffee.

"Thanks, Kitch," Clint said.

Kitchen nodded and withdrew. Clint had the feeling the barman didn't like him, and he wondered if it had to do with Sonya.

"I'll be leaving today," Clint said.

"Really?" Rick said. "You've been here three whole days."

"I got a telegram today," Clint said, "It was from Roxy Doyle."

"Ah, Lady Gunsmith," Rick said. "The protégé I still haven't met."

"One day," Clint said.

"What was on her mind?"

"She's asked me to go to Oklahoma Territory to help Belle Starr."

"The Outlaw Queen?" Rick asked. "Doesn't she have a husband to help her?"

"She does," Clint said, "but apparently she managed to ask Roxy for help, and she can't go."

"Still trying to track down Gavin Doyle?"

"Yep," Clint said.

"So you're doing her a favor."

"Yes." Clint cut into his ham. "I know what you're thinking."

"Hey, no judgments here," Rick said. "She's your friend. I understand. Have you told Sonya, yet?"

"She was with me when I got the telegram, but she doesn't know what it said," Clint said. "I'll tell her."

They finished their breakfast and then Rick went to his office.

"Stop in before you go."

"Right."

Clint picked up his coffee and walked to the bar.

"Am I stepping on your toes, Kitch?"

"How d'ya mean?"

"With Sonya."

"Naw, nothin' happenin' there," Kitchen said. "Not that I wouldn't be interested, ya understand."

"Well, I'm leaving town and probably won't be back for a while," Clint said, "so if you are interested, you'll have a clear field."

"I'll keep that in mind, then," Kitchen said. "Thanks."

"I've got to get my horse ready to travel" Clint said. "I'll be back to say goodbye to her and to Rick."

"I'll tell'er you'll be here."

"Thanks."

He left and headed for the livery.

***

When he had Eclipse saddled and ready, he thought about what Rick had said about getting a new horse.

"You're not ready to head out to pasture, are you, big fella?" Clint asked.

As if he understood the question, the big Darley nodded his head vigorously.

"I didn't think so." Clint mounted up. "Let's go."

Chapter Three

Belle Starr looked at the telegram in her hand. It was from Roxy Doyle, who assured her that help was on the way.

Belle had recently served nine months in prison, thanks to Hanging Judge Isaac Parker of Fort Smith, Arkansas and his marshal, Bass Reeves. However, she had been a model prisoner, and her time had been served fairly easily. On the other hand, her husband, Sam Starr, had been anything but a model prisoner, and had served hard time. As a result, Belle's outlaw tendencies had been softened, while Sam considered himself a hard, bad man, and took every opportunity to prove it.

They lived in a house outside the town of Eufaula, in Oklahoma Indian territory. The town was named after the tribe of the same name. Lately, Sam had been at odds with a local law enforcement official named Frank West. It seemed a forgone conclusion that one was eventually going to kill the other.

But her request for help from Roxy Doyle had nothing to do with that. It was a problem she hadn't even told Sam about, since he was involved with his own hard business. He was her husband and she loved him like crazy, but he was a man and would never think that a woman's trouble was worse than his own—not even his own woman.

She put the telegram from Roxy into her pocket, determined that Sam wouldn't see it when he came in, and just as she did, the door slammed open and he came storming in. A tall, handsome Cherokee who had grown up with the Starr family, he seemed to support the cliché about Indians not handling their fire water, because Sam was a bad drunk.

"That sonofabitch West!" he exploded, slamming the door shut. "I'm gonna kill 'im."

"What did he do now?"

"He's just pushin' me," Sam Starr said, "always pushin' me."

"Sam," Belle said, "you don't wanna end up in prison again."

"I ain't goin' to prison again," he said, firmly, "especially not some prison in Detroit, Michigan. What the hell was Judge Parker thinkin' sendin' us there?" He looked around. "What's for supper?"

"I got a possum stew on the stove," Belle said. She had one hand in her pocket, clutching the telegram from Roxy. "Get yourself washed up."

"Washed up for possum," he complained, going out back to wash up outside.

Belle felt the same way. She wished her husband would go hunting and come home with some real meat, but until he did, it was possum.

Chapter Four

Clint rode into Eufaula, attracting some looks as he passed down the main street. He had been to Oklahoma Indian Territory several times before, and had dealt with both Bass Reeves and Judge Isaac Parker on those occasions. While Parker's court was in Fort Smith, Arkansas, he sent his marshals out into Indian territory to keep the peace, or to track down those who would break it. Clint knew the Starrs were among the lawbreakers, and had even spent some time in jail for it. But according to Roxy, Belle was her friend, so there he was.

He reined in Eclipse in front of the first hotel he spotted and dismounted. After getting himself a room in the Drake Hotel—room seven on the second floor—he got Eclipse settled in a livery, and then went looking for a meal.

He had to find out where Belle and Sam Starr lived, but decided to try to do it without actually asking anybody. If Belle was having trouble with someone, Clint didn't want that person knowing he was here for her—not yet.

He crossed the street to a place called Cajun Café. It was between meals, so he got a table in the back with no trouble.

"Is this for real?" he asked the waiter. "You do Cajun food?"

"Oh, yes sir," the white-haired man said. "Anything you want."

"Do you do Jambalaya?"

"Yes, sir, a very fine Jambalaya."

It wasn't exactly Cajun, but it was New Orleans food, which he liked.

"Okay," he said. "Bring it on."

"Right away, sir. And to drink?"

"Coffee," Clint said, "and bring that out first."

"As you wish."

The coffee was strong, the way Clint liked it, and he drank two cups before his food came out. The Jambalaya had sausage and chicken in it, but no shrimp. That was okay with Clint. He understood the lack of shrimp, considering where they were.

"Thank you."

"Enjoy, sir."

And he did. The food was good, and the café pretty much stayed empty, so he didn't have to deal with people staring at the stranger. When he was finished the waiter asked if he would want dessert, and Clint said no, not this time.

But since the place was empty and there was only the waiter, he decided to change his tactic and try asking a question.

"I understand Belle Starr lives somewhere around here."

"That's right, sir. Do you know her?"

"No, no, I've just heard of her," Clint said. "You know, the 'Bandit Queen' and all."

"Not so much, anymore, sir," the waiter said. "Not since she got out of jail and came back here."

"I see," Clint said. "Did they beat it out of her?"

"Oh no, sir," the waiter said. "From what I've heard she didn't do hard time, at all. It was pretty easy. But, you know, it was still prison."

"I understand," Clint said. "Does she live in town?"

"No, sir, she and her husband have a house outside of town."

"I see."

"I can't tell you exactly where her house is," the man went on, "I've never been there, myself."

"I understand. Thank you for what you did tell me. And thanks for the fine supper."

"It's our pleasure, sir," the waiter said. "Ya'll come back, ya hear?"

He didn't think the man was actually from New Orleans, that was the first time he had heard any Southern accent, and he felt sure it was put on.

He decided to save any questions for somebody who might actually know the answers.

That was usually a bartender.

***

He chose a saloon called The Last Race Saloon. As he entered, he attracted the eyes of most of the patrons. He understood. This was Indian Territory. They had to be wary of strangers, since many riders chose to enter Indian Territory when they were trying to get away from Judge Parker's deputy marshals.

He ignored them and walked to the bar.

"Beer," he said to the bartender.

"Yeah," the sour-faced man said. He drew the beer and set it in front of Clint. "Two bits."

Clint started to lift the brew to his lips, but the bartender put his hand on his wrist, stopping him.

"Before you take a sip."

Clint studied the man, then moved his hand away, took out two bits and dropped it on the bar.

"Enjoy," the man said, picking up the coins.

Chapter Five

Clint nursed the beer and listened to some of the conversations going on around him.

The bartender came over at one point and asked, "Who you tryin' to find?"

"Who says I'm trying to find anybody?"

"Don't kid a kidder, friend," the bartender said. "You been here the better part of an hour and you're workin' on the same beer. And you're listening to everythin' goin' on around ya. You're either a lawman or a bounty hunter."

"Neither," Clint said, "but you're right. I am looking for somebody."

"I knew it!" the barman said, triumphantly. "You want a cold one? On the house?"

"Sure."

The bartender took away the remnants of Clint's warm beer and brought him a cold one in a sweaty mug.

"Thanks."

"Who ya lookin' for?" the man asked, leaning on the bar. "Maybe I can help."

"Why would you?" Clint asked.

"Let's just say I get bored," the bartender said. "My name's Nick Lidgett."

Clint did not offer his name.

"I'm looking to find Belle Starr."

Lidgett's eyebrows went up.

"And you're not a lawman or bounty hunter?"

"She's not wanted at the moment, is she?" Clint asked.

"Not that I know of," Lidgett said. "In fact, she recently got out of prison."

"Right," Clint said. "So no, I'm not a bounty hunter or a lawman. A friend of mine, who's a friend of Belle Starr's, asked me to look her up."

"And what about Sam?"

"Her husband?"

"He's kind of the jealous type," Lidgett said. "And lately he's been drinkin' a lot."

"Here?" Clint asked.

"Here and some other saloons," the bartender said. "You're gonna have to watch out for him."

"Well, all I want to do with Belle is talk," Clint said. "There's no reason for Sam Starr to get jealous about that."

"Actually, you may not have to worry about Sam, after all," Lidgett said.

"Why's that?"

"He's been tanglin' with our local lawman, Frank West."

"Lawman?" Clint asked. "Here in Indian Territory? Is he a marshal?"

"No, no nothing like that," Lidgett said. "The town calls him a constable."

"Well, maybe I should talk to this constable," Clint said. "Just to stay on his good side."

"Frank West don't have a good side," Lidgett said.

"Well then, maybe you can tell me where to find Belle Starr, Nick."

"I have an idea where their house is," Lidgett said, "although I've never been there."

"Do you know anybody who *has* been there?" Clint asked.

"No, but I may be able to find someone," Lidgett said.

"Why don't you just give me your best guess how to get there?" Clint asked. "I'll do the rest."

"Well, if you ride east of town . . ."

***

Clint finished his second beer after Lidgett was done with his directions. It sounded like a bit of the ride, so he was going to have to wait until morning to go looking for Belle.

He thanked Nick Lidgett for the beer, and the information, and left the saloon.

No sooner had he left, Lidgett waved one of his customers over.

"Yeah, Nick?"

Lidgett looked at Jebediah Dixon and said, "You better find Sam Starr and give him a message."

"You want me to find Sam Starr?" Jeb Dixon asked. "On purpose?"

"That's right."

"Why would I do that?"

"Because that fella who just left is lookin' for Sam's wife."

"So?"

Lidgett reached out and put his hand behind Dixon's neck, yanked him forward.

"Sam needs to know."

"Why?" Dixon asked, trying to get away, unsuccessfully.

"Because that fella who just left is Clint Adams," Lidgett said.

He released his hold on Dixon, who just stared.

"The Gunsmith?"

"That's right."

"Are you sure?"

"I recognize him from when I was in Abilene ten years ago. It's him, all right."

"And what's he want with Belle Starr?"

21

"I don't know," Lidgett said, "but maybe Sam's gonna wanna ask him."

"Yeah," Dixon said, "okay . . . but Nick."

"Yeah, Jeb?"

"Where is Sam?"

Chapter Six

Eufaula wasn't much of a town. It had a couple of other, smaller saloons, another café, two hotels and some stores like a mercantile and a hardware store. And, as far as Clint knew, a lawman who wasn't really a lawman, but a sort of self-appointed constable.

Clint wasn't looking forward to meeting this Frank West, so he decided to avoid it, if he could. All he needed to do was find Belle Starr and tell her that Roxy sent him, and then listen to her. And if he could avoid crossing paths with Sam Starr, he'd do that, as well.

After leaving the Last Race Saloon, he went directly to his hotel room. It was starting to get dark, so he figured he'd just sack out, get some rest, and an early start in the morning.

***

Belle Starr cleaned the plates off the table while Sam went outside to have a cigar. That suited her, because as much as she loved him, lately she didn't want to talk to him. That was why she sent telegrams around looking for Roxy Doyle. She needed to talk to the Lady Gunsmith.

Roxy would be able to help her, hopefully without getting Sam involved.

"Belle," Sam yelled from outside, "you bringin' coffee out here?"

"On my way!" Belle snapped.

She didn't know how she had gone from being the Outlaw Queen to Sam's cook and servant, but for now she would bring him coffee, since it might just sober him up.

***

"No sign of him in town," Jeb Dixon told Nick Lidgett.

"You were out there for an hour," the bartender said.

"This ain't a big town, Nick."

"What about his house?"

Dixon shook his head.

"I ain't goin' to Sam and Belle Starr's house," he said. "You wanna do that? Be my guest. They don't like people bein' out there."

"But you know where it is, right?"

"You don't?"

"Just east of town," Lidgett said.

"Did you tell Adams that?"

"Well, yeah," the bartender said, "but I thought you'd get to Sam, first."

"Yeah, well," Dixon said, "let Adams go out there. They'll blow his head off."

"You think so?"

Dixon shrugged.

"Or he'll blow theirs off," he said. "Can I get a beer?"

***

"I'm sorry," Sam said to Belle.

"For what?"

They were sitting together on the top step of their porch, shoulders touching.

"I know I been drinkin' too much," Sam said, "doin' things I shouldn't be doin'."

"Like what?"

Sam looked at Belle. He was thinking about his trips to the whorehouse, but he didn't want to tell her that.

"You know, this thing with Frank West."

"One of you is gonna kill the other," she said. "You know that, don't ya?"

"I know it."

"Unless you stop," she went on. "Just leave him be."

"Me?" Sam said. "Tell him to leave me be!"

"He's just tryin' to make a name for himself, Sam," she said. "The man who tamed Sam Starr. Or maybe even killed him. Don't give him that."

She leaned in and put her head on his shoulder.

"I know, I know," Starr said. "It's just that . . . I did a lot of thinkin' in that Detroit prison. It was like Judge Parker was sayin' we weren't nobody, we didn't deserve to be sent to Yuma prison, we just deserved Detroit. Jesus . . . we was the King and Queen of Outlaws, Belle."

Belle knew that she had been called the Outlaw Queen for years, but never heard Sam called the King. She kept that thought to herself, though.

"You know what we gotta do?" Sam asked.

"What's that, Sam?"

"We gotta reclaim our crowns! We gotta pull a job, the kind the James Boys or the Youngers could never have pulled."

She removed her head from his shoulder and said, "Jesus, Sam . . ."

"What?"

"You wanna go back to prison?" she asked. "Maybe this time more embarrassin'—like Indiana, maybe? Or Florida?"

"We ain't goin' to prison ever again, Belle," Sam said. "We're either gonna pull the biggest job in history or die tryin'!"

Chapter Seven

Clint went back to the Cajun Café for breakfast the next morning.

"Welcome back," the waiter said, as Clint entered. There was only one other person seated at a table.

"Have I beat the breakfast rush?" Clint asked.

"This is the breakfast rush, cher," the waiter said, with a smile. "The people around here aren't used to us, yet. Take any table."

Clint chose the furthest one from the front door and window.

"How did you get here?" he asked. "I mean, from New Orleans."

"Me and my friend thought it was time to travel," he said. "We ran out of money here."

"Then how did you get this place?"

"We won it," the man said. "That is, my friend did, in a poker game. And here we are."

"And where's your friend?"

"He's the cook," the waiter said. "My name is Bruno, and he is Just."

"Just?"

"That is his name," Bruno said, with a shrug.

"Swell," Clint said, "this is Oklahoma Territory. The people here are more used to eating like Indians than French Cajuns."

"We have discovered that."

"But they don't know what they're missing," Clint said. "How about some Cajun hash?"

"Ah, excellent choice!" Bruno said, happily. "I will tell Just. And coffee?"

"Yes."

"With chicory?"

"Of course."

As Bruno went to the kitchen, Clint looked over at the other people's table. It was a man and a woman in their forties—probably married, because they weren't talking much—and they seemed to have simple ham-and-eggs on their plate. At that moment, the woman looked over at him and smiled.

"You've got to try a Cajun breakfast, next time," Clint said. "It's delicious."

"We don't know—" the woman stared, but the man cut her off abruptly.

"Lucy!" She snapped her mouth closed. "We don't need to discuss our breakfast with no stranger."

She looked down at her plate, but when the man started eating again, she stole another glance at Clint. When he smiled, she looked away.

Bruno returned from the kitchen, carrying a tray bearing a plate, a pot and a mug. As he walked across the floor, Clint realized that, despite the white hair, he was not an old man, forties, perhaps, but not old.

He set the items down on the table, and the smell of the eggs, Andouille, red-skinned potatoes, peppers, onions and mushrooms caused his stomach to growl with anticipation. In addition, the spices in the dish made his mouth water.

"Please, enjoy it as much as Just enjoyed cooking it," Bruno said.

"Tell him thank you for me," Clint said.

He sipped the coffee first, found it strong and laced with just the right amount of chicory. Then he dug his fork into the hash. The spices came alive in his mouth, the eggs and sausage merged together as he chewed. Bruno returned with a basket of bread.

"Beignets," he said. "And fresh."

"They look great." Much better than the usual biscuits he had for breakfast—light, but not flaky, covered with white powdered sugar.

"You pay the bill," he heard the man say to the woman at the other table. "I have to go open the store."

"I'll see you later, then," she said.

"Have supper ready," he said. "I'll need some real American food after eating this slop."

"It was just ham-and-eggs" she said, but he stormed out without looking back. She stared down at the table, as if ashamed.

Clint felt sorry for the woman. He was watching her when she lifted her eyes and looked at him. She smiled, and he saw for the first time how lovely she was. Not a child, in her thirties, a mature beauty.

"That smells wonderful," she said to him.

"Come over and have a taste," he invited.

"Oh, I couldn't . . ." she said, but he saw how curious she was.

"Come on," he said. "I'll even have Bruno bring out some more, if you like it."

She thought a moment, then took a deep breath, stood up and walked over. Clint got up and held the other chair for her, then sat back down.

"I'll get a fork from your table—" he started to offer.

"No need," she said. "I'll use yours."

She leaned forward, and he knew that she wanted him to feed her. He took a good portion onto his fork, with all the ingredients on it, and fed it into her open, waiting mouth. She chewed and her eyes went wide.

"Do you want me to have him bring you some?" he asked.

She swallowed and said, "Oh, yes."

Chapter Eight

At one point, Bruno was standing there, watching with pleasure as they both ate.

"Where do you get these ingredients?" Clint asked. "You can't be growing them out here."

"Once every few months we have them delivered from Kansas City to Fort Smith. Then we go to Fort Smith with a wagon and pick them up. That is, we have someone do it for us."

Two men came into the café and Bruno excused himself.

"You were telling me why you're here," the woman reminded him.

After Clint asked Bruno to bring her a plate, they had exchanged names. She was Ashley Givens, and her husband was Hank. He ran the local mercantile—which, by the way, did not carry the ingredients Just needed for his Cajun dishes.

"I was saying that I'm just passing through," he reminded her.

"Here?" she asked. "On your way to where? The only reason we're here is that our wagon broke down. We were stuck, and then Hank found out that the mercantile was for sale and . . . bang. We live here."

"And do you work in the store with him?"

"No," she said, "neither of us wants that. I don't need that yelling all day long, I get enough of it at home."

"Why put up with it?" he asked.

"Where am I gonna go?" she asked. "Believe me, I'm stuck here." She put another forkful of hash into her mouth. "My God, I've got to find out how he makes this."

"And if you make it for Hank," Clint asked, "won't he wonder how you knew how to do it?"

"Yes." Her shoulders slumped. "If he knew I was here right now eating this with you, he'd tan me good."

"Does he do that?" Clint asked. "Beat you?"

"Oh, no," she said, "not beatings. I mean, he's hit me once or twice, but . . ." She shrugged.

Clint decided to change the subject.

"So how long have you lived here?"

"Just a few months."

"Do you know Sam and Belle Starr?"

"Oh, of course," she said. "Everybody around here knows them."

"I'm trying to find Belle," he said. "A friend of mine asked me to look her up. I just don't know where she lives. The bartender at the Last Race gave me some directions, but they're vague and I don't think he really knows, either."

"Oh, I do," she said.

"You do?"

"Sure," she said. "Hank makes deliveries there, some-times."

"Then you know how to get there."

"Yes, I do."

"Could you tell me?" he asked.

"Oh," she said, "if I did that, I'd probably get into a lot of trouble. The Starrs are very private people."

"I understand that," he said, "but it's important I talk to Belle."

She chewed her food and stared across the table at him. He noticed a change in her expression.

"I could," she said.

"But will you?" he asked.

"Well," she asked, giving him a coy look, "what's in it for me?"

"You mean this meal isn't enough?" he asked.

"It's delicious," she said, "don't get me wrong, but to take a chance of getting the Starrs and Hank mad at me, there's going to have to be something else."

"Like what?"

"You said your name is Clint Adams?"

"That's right."

"So that makes you the Gunsmith, huh?"

"Right again."

"You're kind of a gentleman, given the reputation you have."

"You can't always believe a reputation."

"I know that," she said. "Belle Starr doesn't seem to live up to hers, either."

"Worse?"

"Better," she said. "But Sam . . . he's kind of an angry drunk."

"That's too bad."

"He drinks with Hank sometimes."

"Is that a fact?"

"And Hank comes home and falls into bed, goes right to sleep."

"I see."

"You see what I'm getting at?" she asked. "Hank and me, we don't have much sex."

"That's too bad."

"But you have more than one reputation, you know," she pointed out.

"And which one do you want to make use of?" he asked.

"I was just wondering," she said, putting her fork down, "do you have a hotel room?"

Chapter Nine

On one hand, Clint didn't think he had time for Ashley. He had to go out and find Belle Starr. On the other hand, this woman claimed to know where Belle was, and she just wanted something from him before she told him.

"Yes," he said, "I have a hotel room."

"Then what are we waiting for?" she asked.

"What about your husband?" Clint asked.

"Oh, he's at the store," she said, "and he's the only one there, so he'll be busy all day."

"And you really know how to get to Belle Starr's house?"

"I really do know."

"All right, then," he said. "Let's go."

"You better go first," she said. "Just tell me what hotel, and what room, and I'll follow."

"Okay," he said, "I'm room seven at the Drake."

"That's the best hotel in town," she said.

"Is it?"

"Although that's not saying much in this town."

"Let me get this check, and then I'll go, and see you there."

He stood up.

"Don't look like you're going to the gallows, Clint."

***

Clint couldn't remember the last time he had felt he was being forced into sex with a woman. Usually, he was all for it. Although he spent many years avoiding married women, in the past few years women—married or not—seemed to be getting more and more aggressive about sex. This was a perfect example—a married woman, unhappy with her life taking the opportunity to make a change, at least for one afternoon.

He went to his hotel, got the bed ready in his room, then sat on it to wait. It was his hope that she wasn't lying about knowing where Belle Starr could be found, but he'd find out about that after.

When the knock came at the door—three quick, soft sounds—he stood and, still wearing his holster, walked to it.

"Who is it?"

"Let me in before somebody sees me!" Ashley's voice hissed, urgently.

He opened the door a crack, made sure it was her and she was alone, then quickly let her in.

She looked flushed as she studied him.

"You're not going to need that gunbelt," she said.

He walked to the bed, removed the belt and hung it on the bed post.

"Okay, I get it," she said. "You have to keep it close."

"Let's get started," he said, unbuttoning his shirt.

"Whoa, whoa," she said. "I'm not rushing this. I want to enjoy every minute. And I'll make it worth your while."

"By telling me where to find Belle Starr."

She smiled and said, "That, too."

Slowly, she undid all the buttons down the front of her dress, and then peeled it off. Next came the array of underthings women wore, which eventually ended up being all over the room.

And then she was naked—tall, high breasted, long-legged.

"And now you," she said.

She watched, an amused look on her face, as he disrobed. As his hard penis came into view, the look changed from amusement to lust.

"Oh," she said, simply.

"You're not so bad, yourself," he said.

They moved at the same time, stepping forward, into each other's arms. Their mouths came together, his willing hers insistent and hungry. She ran her hands over his back, brought them down to his buttocks, where she dug her nails in. Between them, his cock kept getting harder and longer. Finally, she couldn't ignore it any longer. She broke the kiss, fell to her knees and gave his penis all of her attention. She brought her hands around from behind him and fondled it for several moments. Then she pressed it to her cheek, feeling the smoothness of the hot flesh.

"Beautiful," she said. "My husband's is an ugly, veiny thing."

Before he could say anything, she took him into her mouth and began to suck and taste him, swirling her tongue around him.

She enjoyed the smoothness on her lips and tongue, and spent a long time on it. When she finally released him from her mouth, he was gleaming with her saliva.

She stood then, took both his hands, and led him to the bed. They got on it together, and he lowered her onto her back. He began to roam her body with his hands and mouth, kissing first her mouth again, then her neck, shoulders, and breasts. He spent time on each nipple, teasing and biting them until they stood out, the dark brown of them in stark contrast to her pale skin.

As he worked her breasts with his mouth, he slid his hand down between her thighs, worked her with his fingers until she was wet and slick.

Normally, he would have moved down there with his mouth and tasted her, but he didn't feel he had the time to spend, so instead he mounted her, and drove his cock into her, brutally. He fucked her, then, with such force that she couldn't speak, couldn't do anything but make grunting sounds while lifting her hips to meet each thrust . . .

Chapter Ten

As Clint got dressed, she said, "I'm not done with you, yet."

"I'm done," he said. "I have things to do."

She rolled onto her stomach and looked up at him. His eyes went to the twin mounds of her tight butt.

"I don't," she said. "Nothing at all—well, until later, when my husband comes home."

"Then what do you do?" he asked.

She made a face.

"Wifely things," she said. "Make supper, then let him rut on top of me until he rolls off and goes to sleep."

"Doesn't sound like a good life."

"It isn't," she said. "I wasn't cut out to be a wife. At least, not to a man like Hank."

"Then leave him."

"And go where?" she asked. "My choices are very limited."

"I wish I could help," he said, "but now it's time for you to keep your word."

"My word?"

"Tell me were Belle Starr lives."

"Oh, that." She allowed her eyes to slide away from his.

"Did you lie to me?" he asked. "You don't know where I can find her?"

"Well," she said, "not exactly. I've never been there, but Hank's gone several times. After the first time he told me where it was, but then he never talked about it, again."

"But you have some idea of where it might be?"

"It's a house, I know that," she said, "and it's west of town."

The bartender had told Clint that it was east of town. Obviously, he had lied.

"Okay, a house west of town," he said. "What else?"

"It's in front of a hill that has two peaks, Hank said," she added. "That's all I know."

"A hill with two peaks," he said. "That might be of help." He went to the bedpost, retrieved his gunbelt and put it on. "You better get dressed."

"Are you sure you have to go now?" she asked.

"Yes," he said, "I'm sorry. This was very . . . pleasant."

"Yes, it was, wasn't it," she said. "But you rushed it, didn't you?"

"Kind of," he admitted. "I'm sorry."

"Don't be," she said. "It was still better than anything I've experienced before with a man. Thank you."

"Do you want me to walk you anywhere?" he asked.

"No, no," she said, "I can get around town with no problem. But . . ."

"Yes?"

"Do you mind if I lay here a while," she said. "Like I said, I've got nowhere to go and nothing to do."

"That's fine," he said. "I'll leave the key. Just lock the door when you leave, and then drop the key at the desk."

"All right."

He went to the door.

"Clint?"

He turned.

"Can we do this again?"

"Ashley . . . I don't know," he said. "I don't know how long I'm going to be here."

"Well," she said, rolling onto her back so he could see her breasts, "I'm available."

He stared, then turned away and said, "I'll keep that in mind."

He left the room.

***

Clint walked to the livery where he'd left Eclipse with a hostler who was as impressed as they all were. Most of these men actually loved horses, and when they saw one like the Darley, Clint knew they'd take good care of his animal.

"He's real chipper," the man said. "Ate all his feed. I think he's rarin' to go, again."

"Good," Clint said. "We're going for a short run."

"Will you be bringin' him back?" the man asked, hopefully.

"Very likely."

"Good. Uh, where are you headed?" the man asked. "You need directions?"

Clint studied the man, who appeared to be in his fifties.

"Have you lived here long?"

"Longer than most."

"Do you know . . ." Clint trailed off, then changed the question rather than mention Belle Star. "Do you know where there's a hill around here that has two peaks? Maybe west of town?"

The man grinned.

"You're talkin' about the twin peaks."

"That's a fancy name for a hill."

The man shrugged.

"It's got two peaks, what else wouldja call it?"

"What's your name?" Clint asked.

"Shorty Anderson," the man said.

"Well, Shorty," Clint asked, "how do I get to twin peaks?"

"Well," Shortly said, "I'll tell ya . . ."

Chapter Eleven

Sam Starr rose that morning and had breakfast with Belle.

"I'm goin' out," he said, when they had finished.

"Where?" she asked.

"Just out."

"When will you be back?"

"I don't know," he said. "Later tonight."

Before she could ask anything else, he was out the front door. He circled around the house to the corral in the back and saddled his horse. Belle's horse watched without moving much but her head.

Starr saddled his mount and climbed aboard, taking a moment to stare at the twin peaks behind the house. Then he spurred his horse on, and headed out.

Belle watched from the front window, wondering if Sam was going off to sleep with somebody, or rob somebody or, maybe, kill?

***

Clint followed the directions he'd gotten from both Ashley and Shorty, ignored what he had gotten from the bartender. Before long he could see the twin peaks Shorty had told him about. He headed for them, and eventually saw the small house with the corral behind it.

If only Belle Starr was inside, he figured he'd be able to avoid trouble, but if Sam Starr was around . . . Then he noticed there was only one horse in the corral.

He decided to dismount and approach on foot, walking Eclipse in. He hoped this would make him appear non-threatening. As he approached the house, the front door opened and a woman holding a rifle stepped out. She had dark hair, a trim figure, wasn't particularly pretty.

"Stop right there!" she snapped.

He stopped, because attractive or not, she was pointing a gun at him.

"What do you want?" she demanded.

"Well, if you're Belle Starr," he said, "then you . . . that is, I want to talk to you."

"Talk from there, Mister," she said, "and make it quick. This trigger finger's got an itch I need to scratch."

"Roxy Doyle sent me."

Belle Starr hesitated, then said, "W-what?

"Apparently, you sent her a message asking for help, and she couldn't come, so she sent me."

"And who are you?"

"The name's Clint Adams."

"The Gunsmith?"

"That's right."

She lowered the rifle and asked, "Why didn't you say so in the first place? Tie off your horse and come inside."

"I don't have to tie him," Clint said, dropping Eclipse's lead, "he won't go anywhere."

"Suit yourself," Belle Starr said. "Come on in. I got some coffee goin'."

***

"Say that again," Sam Starr said to Jebediah Dixon.

"He's been lookin' for ya, Sam," Dixon said. "Nick Lidgett says there's a fella in town lookin' for you."

"What for?" Starr asked. "I ain't done nothin'."

"He don't know," Dixon said. "He just says the fella was looking for Belle."

"Belle or me?" Starr asked. "Make up your mind?"

"I dunno." They were standing in front of the whore-house. Dixon had caught Starr as he was coming out. "I think he said Belle."

"Christ!" Starr said. "I better get home. Tell Nick to keep an eye out."

"I will."

Starr walked to his horse tied nearby, mounted up and rode off. Instead of going straight to the Last Race Saloon to deliver Starr's message, Dixon decided to go into the whorehouse.

***

Bell Starr sat at her kitchen table with a cup of coffee, stared across at Clint.

"Is that coffee all right?"

"It's fine," Clint said. "Good, in fact. Thanks."

"So where's Roxy?" Belle asked. "Still off tryin' to find her father?"

"Always," Clint said. "That girl never gives up."

"Well," Belle said, "I suppose I should be grateful she sent you. She told me a lot about you when we first met. All of it good."

"That's nice to hear," Clint said. "Now, suppose you tell me something."

"Why I asked for her help?" she asked. "There's a story there."

"I'm all ears," he said.

Chapter Twelve

"Judge Isaac Parker sent me to prison . . ."

"I know that."

". . . in Detroit, Michigan."

"Oh," he said. "That I didn't know. Why Michigan?"

"I think it was because nobody there knew who I was," Belle said. "They were intimidated by my 'Outlaw Queen' reputation—which is crap, by the way."

"Most reputations are."

"Is yours?"

He hesitated, then said, "Somewhat."

"Well, he sent me and Sam there, and we each had our own experiences," Belle said. "When we came home, we didn't talk about them, and we still don't."

"So you need Roxy to . . . what? Talk to?"

"I need more than that," she said.

He decided to keep quiet and let her get to it. But at that moment, they both heard a horse gallop up to the house and stop.

"Oh shit," she said. "That'd be Sam."

"Is there going to be a problem?" he asked.

She bit her lip and said, "Probably."

The door slammed open and Sam Starr stepped in. He was not a tall man, but his anger seemed to make him taller.

"What the hell is goin' on?" he demanded.

Clint decided to remain calm.

"I'm having a cup of coffee with your wife," he said.

"Oh, yeah? Why?"

"She offered."

Sam stared at Belle.

"What else did you offer him?"

"Don't be an ass, Sam," she said. "You remember Roxy Doyle?"

"That snooty bitch, Lady Gunsmith? Sure, I remember her. Why?"

"This is Clint Adams, her friend," Belle said. "She asked him to look in on us if he was in the area."

Not exactly true, but Clint had no choice but to go along with the story.

"That's right," he said. "So I rode up, and your wife pointed a rifle at me until I told her who I was. That's when she offered me a cup of coffee."

Sam frowned at Clint.

"Was you in town lookin' for me?" he demanded.

"I was in town looking for Belle Starr," Clint said. "Is that the same thing?"

"Belle," Sam said, "get me a cup of coffee."

Belle stood up and did as her husband asked. She did it in a docile manner, which was not the Belle Starr that Roxy Doyle had once described to Clint. Roxy had said she was "fierce" and a "fighter." That was not the woman Clint was seeing today.

Sam Starr walked to the table and sat.

"And put some whiskey in mine!" he snapped.

She brought him a cup of coffee and a bottle of whiskey, so he could doctor his own brew.

"Is the Doyle woman still callin' herself Lady Gunsmith?" Sam asked.

"Others are," Clint said.

"Doesn't that get your goat, havin' her use your name like that?"

"Gunsmith is not my name," Clint said. "And whatever Roxy wants to do is fine with me."

Sam sipped his whiskey-doctored coffee before speaking again.

"So you're one of the men she's leadin' around by his pecker?"

"The lady happens to be a friend of mine," Clint said. "You disrespect her one more time and I'll have to put your head through a window."

Belle made a sound Clint thought might have been the beginning of a laugh, but then she stifled it.

"Really?" Sam Starr asked. "Not shoot me?"

"Sam," Clint said, "I wouldn't need my gun to take care of the likes of you."

Sam Starr's face suffused with blood at the insult.

"Adams," he said, "you better get the hell outta my house."

"With pleasure," Clint said.

He stood, looked at Belle.

"I'm sorry our talk was cut short, Belle," he said.

"Give Roxy my love," Belle said.

"I will," he said, "when I leave town, which will probably be in a couple of days."

"You got business here?" Sam Starr asked.

"I happen to like this town," Clint said. "Thought I'd just stay a while."

"In Indian Territory?"

"I've got another friend who works around here," Clint said. "Maybe you know him? Bass Reeves?"

Starr stood up, his body taut with rage.

"I don't wanna see you or Reeves around here, understand?" he said.

"Belle," Clint said, nodding to her. "A pleasure."

He left.

Chapter Thirteen

Clint rode back to town, hoping Belle Starr had gotten his message and would come to see him. Or, at least, contact him.

As he rode into town, he saw a black man sitting in a chair in front of his hotel. He also saw the badge glistening on the man's chest. He rode his horse over to him, instead of to the livery.

"Bass," he said.

"Clint."

"Funny, I was just talking about you."

"That a fact?" Reeves asked. "Who to?"

"Sam and Belle Starr."

Reeves stood up.

"What brings you to town?" Clint asked.

"I heard you were in the area," Reeves said. "Thought I'd come over and ask why. Only, maybe now I know."

"Why don't we go and get a drink?" Clint suggested. "Mind if I take care of my horse first?"

"Nope," Reeves said. "I'll see you over at the Last Race."

As Reeves started to walk away Clint said, "Hey?"

"Yeah?"

"Do you know the bartender there? Nick Lidgett?"

"Yeah, I know 'im."

"He friends with Sam Starr?"

"So they say."

Clint nodded.

"Okay, thanks. See you there."

Reeves walked one way, while Clint rode the other.

***

As Clint walked into the Last Race, he saw Reeves seated at a table way in the back of the almost empty saloon. Then he looked at the bar, where the bartender, Lidgett, was standing with a sour look. Clint walked over and asked for a beer.

"Where is everybody?" he asked.

"They walked out when Bass Reeves walked in," Lidgett said. "Why are you here?"

"To see Reeves," Clint said.

Lidgett pushed a beer over to him.

"See if you can get him to leave and the beer's on the house."

"I'll keep that in mind."

***

When James F. Fagen was appointed Marshal by Judge Isaac Parker, he was ordered to hire two hundred deputies to cover Western Arkansas District—which included Indian Territory. One of the first he hired was Bass Reeves, who went from being a farmer to the first black marshal, mainly because of his knowledge of the Indian Territory. Reeves was in his mid-forties now, a serious looking man who sported a long, drooping mustache that contributed to that demeanor.

Clint carried his beer to Reeves' table and sat down. Reeves' beer was still half full.

"What's this about the Starrs?" Reeves asked. "Are they wanted somewhere else?"

"Not that I know of."

"Then what are you doin' talkin' to them?"

"I was asked by a friend to talk to Belle Starr," Clint said. "Sam just happened to come home before we were finished."

"And did he make trouble?"

"He acted tough," Clint said, "but nothing happened."

"I'd watch my back if I was you," Reeves said. "What's this thing with Belle?"

"I don't know," Clint said. "She reached out to Roxy Doyle for help. Roxy couldn't respond, so she asked me to come by. That's what I was doing there when Sam walked in. I didn't get a chance to hear the problem, but I let her know I'd be around."

"Well," Reeves said, "Judge Parker and Marshal Fagen want Belle and Sam Starr gone. You mind keepin' me informed about what's goin' on with you and them?"

"Not at all," Clint said. "As long as it doesn't interfere with what Roxy asked me to do."

"Fair enough."

Reeves finished his beer and stood up, put his black hat on.

"I'll be on my way," he said, "but I'll check back. You get anythin' for me, you can contact Marshal Fagen in Fort Smith. He'll get the information to me."

"I'll do that, Bass," Clint said. "Good seeing you."

"You, too, Clint," Reeves said. "And here's a warnin' for ya—Marshal Fagen'll try to sign you up when he knows you're here."

"I think I'll be able to resist," Clint said. "That badge looks too heavy for me."

Reeves looked down at the hunk of medal pinned to his shirt.

"Yeah," he said, "sometimes it's kinda too heavy for me, too."

Chapter Fourteen

Clint finished his beer, then went back up to the bar.

"Thanks for gettin' him outta here," Lidgett said. "Another one on the house?"

"Sure, why not?"

Lidgett set him up with a mug.

"Did you find Belle Starr?" Lidgett asked.

"Belle and Sam," Clint said. "But not where you told me. Funny, it was exactly the opposite."

"That a fact?" Lidgett said. "I musta been wrong."

"Yeah, you must've."

"So what happened with Sam?"

"Not much," Clint said. "He tried to get tough, but I think I cured him of that."

"Really?"

"Doesn't that sound like Starr?" Clint asked.

"Now how would I know that?" Lidgett asked.

"Well, I heard you and Starr are friends."

"More like acquaintances," Lidgett said. "If we were friends, I wouldn't have got the information about where he lives wrong, would I?"

"If you were his friend, you definitely would have sent me off on a wild goose chase."

"Now look," Lidgett said, "I'm just a bartender."

"Right," Clint said. "Thanks for the beers." He pushed the second one away, untouched. "See you around."

He turned and left the saloon, just as several customers were coming in.

"Is Reeves gone?" he heard one of them yell . . .

***

Clint decided to stay visible on the street, in case Belle Starr came looking for him. He went to his hotel and sat in the chair Bass Reeves had been in. He figured if Belle could get away from her husband, she'd come riding in.

After he was seated there about an hour, with people eyeing him as they went by, a man crossed the street toward him. As he got closer, Clint could see the tarnished metal on his chest, too dull to reflect light.

"Mr. Adams?" the man asked. He was tall, slender, wearing a gun on his right hip.

"That's right."

"My name's Frank West," the man said, "Constable West."

"Constable," Clint said. "Is there anything I can do for you?"

"Yeah," West said, "you can tell me what your interest in Sam Starr is."

"I have no interest in Sam Starr at all," Clint said.

"I understood you were lookin' for him."

"Who told you that?"

"I have my sources in town."

"Well, your sources were wrong," Clint said.

"So you're claimin' you were never lookin' for Sam Starr?" West asked.

"That's right."

West studied him, then brightened.

"I get it," he said. "You were lookin' for Belle."

Clint didn't answer.

"I need an answer, Adams."

"Tell me, Constable," Clint said, "where does your authority come from?"

"From this," West said, touching his badge.

"But you didn't get that from Judge Isaac Parker, in Fort Smith, did you?"

"No, but—"

"So then you have no jurisdiction here," Clint said. "You can't ask me questions."

"I back my questions up with this," West said, tapping the badge again, "and with this," he added, touching his gun.

"Not this time, Constable," Clint said. "I'll talk to Judge Parker, Marshal Fagan, or even Deputy Marshal Reeves. Not with you."

"Are you tryin' to test my authority?"

"No," Clint said, "since you have none. You're a self-appointed man looking for some authority where it doesn't exist."

"This town believes in my authority."

"Well. Lucky I'll be leaving this town any day now," he said. "Whataya think of that?"

"If I find out you've been breaking the law in my town," West said, "I'll put you in a cell before you can leave. Got it?"

"Oh, I get it, now," Clint said. "You like to flex your muscles. Well, as far as I'm concerned, you have no muscles to flex. Not with me."

"Just remember what I said, Mr. Adams," Frank West reminded him.

"I'll remember it," Clint said.

West hesitated, then turned and walked back across the street.

Chapter Fifteen

Clint sat in front of the hotel for several hours, then decided Belle Starr was not going to come right up to him. She might get away from Sam Starr for a couple of hours, but they'd have to meet somewhere off the street.

He wondered where he could put himself so Belle Starr would find him, then decided he had been playing it all wrong. He should have simply waited in his own room.

He quit the chair, went into the hotel and up to his room. At the door he stopped before fitting the key into the lock. Somebody was inside. Ready to produce his weapon in a split second, he unlocked the door and swung it open.

"Where have you been?" Belle Starr asked. "I've been waiting." She was seated on the bed, fully dressed.

"You didn't see me sitting out front?"

"I came in the back way."

He closed the door, took his hand away from his gun.

"I'm unarmed," she said.

"I noticed that," Clint said.

"Can we talk?" she asked. "Sam's gonna be wonder-in' where I am."

He walked to the bed and sat down beside her.

"Talk."

"Somebody's tryin' to kill me."

"Who?"

"I don't know," she said. "I probably should say, somebody is going to try to kill me."

"What makes you say that?"

"When I left prison," she said, "somebody I was serving time with told me it was gonna happen."

"Did they say why?"

"No," Belle said, "just that it was going to happen when I got back here."

"Then why did you come back here?" Clint asked. "Why not go someplace else?"

"Where?" she asked. "This is the only real home I've ever known."

"Did you tell Sam this?"

"I tried," she said, "but Sam's got his own problems. Being in prison in Detroit did somethin' to him and he's tryin' to work through it."

"How?"

"Drinkin', whorin', the way men handle everythin'."

"I get it."

"I was hopin' Roxy would be available to help me."

"You're the Outlaw Queen," Clint said. "Why would you need help?"

"I may steal, but I'm not a fast gun," she said. "I don't have what Roxy has—and what you have—inside. It's natural to the two of you."

"Do you mean killing?"

"I mean, self-preservation," she said, "and the ability to enforce it."

Clint stared at her.

"Yeah, I know," she said, "sometimes I sound smart. I'm not a complete idiot."

"I guess not."

She stood up, turned to face him.

"Will you stay and help me?"

"That's what Roxy asked me to do, help you," Clint said. "So that's what I'll do."

"Then maybe you can help me with somethin' else, too."

"What?"

She suddenly threw herself onto his lap, wrapped her arms around his neck and kissed him. Her breath was hot, her tongue searching, and she smelled like pure sex. His body reacted, in spite of himself.

But he managed to pull his mouth from hers and say, "What the hell—"

She got off his lap and stepped back.

"I'm sorry," she said. "It's been a while since Sam and I . . . He's been spendin' time with whores while I sit at home. I just need . . . a release. And Roxy told me about you, and how you are with a woman."

"Did she now?"

"She said you were gentle, and kind, and lovin'," she said. "I don't think I've ever experienced that in a man. I love Sam, but he's none of those things. Clint . . . I need this."

Her hat was on the bed, and her dark hair was down, hanging past her shoulders. She hastily unbuttoned her shirt, removed it and tossed it away. Her breasts were small, but firm, with pale nipples that almost blended into her pale skin.

She sat on the bed next to him and said, "Can you help me . . ." She raised her feet.

He got off the bed, knelt down and pulled her boots off for her. Then she stood and wriggled out of her Levis and kicked them away. When she was naked, he could smell her readiness even more. At that moment, the woman was exuding pure sex.

She stepped closer, unbuttoned his shirt, ran her hands over his bare chest.

"I can help with your boots," she said.

He sighed helplessly, and sat on the edge of the bed.

Married women . . .

Chapter Sixteen

Clint gathered Belle Starr into his arms and kissed her. She was a rather plain woman, but she tasted good, felt right in his arms, her skin was hot and smooth against his. There was more to women than just looks, a fact he had discovered a long time ago. Some beautiful women were cold and unresponsive, while he had found some unattractive women hot, and lively, full of energy. In bed, they suddenly became sex goddesses, and looks had nothing to do with it.

Such a woman was Belle Starr. As they tumbled onto the bed, her hands roamed all over him, finally taking hold of his hard cock.

She pushed him down onto his back, crouched down between his legs and gobbled his penis up, sucking it avidly. He didn't know how long she had been in prison, or how long she had been out, but a combination of the sentence, and an unresponsive husband, had obviously made her hungry for contact, and she was now making the most of it.

She rubbed her palms over his thighs as she sucked him, then slid her hands beneath him to cup his ass cheeks. With surprising strength, she lifted him as if the act would drive him deeper into her mouth.

When he thought he would explode into her mouth, she suddenly moved one hand to grasp the base of his cock and squeeze, staving off the urge.

"Oh, not yet," she said, "not yet, you beautiful man."

Clint had seen Sam Starr, knew him to be a handsome man. He wondered if Belle ever called him beautiful? Although he knew, since he had heard it from other women, Belle wasn't talking about his face.

She crawled up onto him, settled into his lap, then reached between them to grasp his cock and guide it to her hot, wet vagina. Then she sat down on him, taking him inside with a gasp. She closed her eyes and began riding him up and down, her small breasts bouncing about. He realized this was something he never wanted to tell Roxy about, and hoped Belle wouldn't, either. But he soon stopped thinking about it—or anything, for that matter—except what was going on at the moment. Belle Starr began to bounce on him faster and faster, her head tossed back, the cords on her neck sticking out, and suddenly he felt a gush from her, all slick and wet and aromatic, soaking both him and the sheets beneath them. But despite that, Belle didn't stop moving. She kept going and going, until she did it again, and a third time, and eventually she sucked his ejaculation right out of him, and they both yelled . . .

***

"Oh God," she said, moments later, "I ain't never gushed like that so any times."

They were lying together, but to one side, away from the area of sheets she had soaked with her nectar.

"Roxy didn't tell me about that!"

"Look," Clint said, "I don't know how much Roxy told you, but I wouldn't tell her about this—"

"Oh hell, Clint," she said, "I ain't tellin' nobody about this. This is just between you and me, darlin'."

"Good," he said, "good."

"Jesus," she said, unwrapping her legs from his, "I gotta go. I don't wanna, but I gotta."

She slipped from the bed and he watched as she dressed.

"Uh, Belle . . ."

"Yeah?"

"You smell kind of—well, you know. You want to go home like that?"

"Sam will have drunk himself to sleep by now," she said. "I'll wash up before I get into bed. He'll never know."

She looked around for her hat, which had been kicked from the bed, found it and jammed it onto her head.

"I gotta thank ya, Clint," she said, "I think this may just hold me for a while, until Sam can work out what's botherin' him."

"Belle," he said, "before you go, tell me about Frank West."

"Did you meet Constable West?" She said "constable" like it was a dirty word.

"I did," he said. "He came up to me—"

"Actin' tough?" she asked.

"Well, not tough, exactly—"

"Clint, I'd think Frank West would be afraid of you. He ain't afraid of Sam, and he's always lettin' him know. But I don't think you gotta worry about Frank West."

"He's after Sam?"

"Oh yeah," Belle said, "one of them is gonna kill the other for sure."

"Maybe I could have Bass Reeves have a talk with him."

"I don't care if you talk to him, Clint, but I don't want no help from the likes of Bass Reeves, and neither does Sam. He's the one who arrested us, and we ended up in goddamned Detroit!"

"I'm sure Reeves had nothing to do with where you did your time, Belle," Clint said. "That'd be Judge Parker—"

"You're probably right about that," she said, "but that's how me and Sam feel."

"Okay, then," Clint promised, "no Bass Reeves."

Impulsively, she ran to the bed, kissed him, stroked his penis one last time, and then made for the door.

"Watch your back, Belle," he yelled, "and I'll see what I can find out about this threat to you."

She waved, and went out the door.

Chapter Seventeen

Belle Starr mounted her horse behind Clint Adams' hotel. It was dark, so she doubted anyone would see her leaving town. She rode out and headed for her house, in front of the twin peaks. As she left the road there was a shot, and a burning sensation in her chest. Then she felt herself falling, but did not feel herself hit the ground . . .

***

By morning the sheets had dried, but everything still smelled of Belle Starr. He didn't mind, but it would be distracting to walk around all day with her aroma in his nostrils. Rather than take the time to have a bath, he used the pitcher-and-basin in his room and washed himself as thoroughly as he could.

That done he left the room and the hotel, in search of breakfast. He walked two blocks when he saw a crowd of people gathered around a buckboard across the street. Curious, he crossed over and discovered it was a doctor's office, complete with a shingle outside that said: DOCTOR T. HEWITT.

As he reached the crowd, he asked a man, "What's going on?"

"Somebody found a body," the man said. "They brought it to the doc."

"Where is it?" Clint asked.

"It was in the buckboard, but they carried it into the doc's office."

"So why all the attention?" Clint asked.

"Well," another man said, "it wasn't just a body, was it? It was a woman."

"And it wasn't just a woman," a nearby lady said, "it was Belle Starr."

"What?"

"Yeah," the lady said, "they just took her—hey, where ya goin'?"

Clint pushed through the crowd and entered the doctor's office.

"Doc?" he called. "Where are you?"

"Back here," a voice shouted from another room.

Clint went through the door, saw a man in a white coat and several other men standing around a table. On the table was Belle Starr.

"All right," the doctor said. "All of you out. I've got work to do."

The three men turned and filed past Clint.

"Work?" Clint asked the doctor.

The doctor turned and looked at him.

"I've got to try and save her life," he said. "Who are you?"

"My name's Clint Adams. I'm a friend of Belle's."

"Adams? The Gunsmith?"

"That's right."

The doctor was a tall, older man, wearing wire-framed glasses. He had bushy white eyebrows above clear blue eyes.

"Did you shoot her?"

"What? No, I just said, I'm a friend."

"Well, if that's the case you'll get out of here and let me try to save her."

"How many times was she shot."

"Twice, in the chest. Oh, hey, if you want to do something, find Sam Starr. Tell him what happened and get him here."

"I can do that." Clint looked at Belle. The front of her shirt was soaked with blood. "You better get to it. She doesn't look good."

"She must've been lying out there all night," the doctor said. "You better get Sam here fast, just in case."

"Right," Clint said. "I'm on my way."

***

Clint hurried to the livery, saddled Eclipse and rode him out to the house Belle shared with her husband. Last night she had said Sam would have drunk himself to sleep. Clint only hoped he'd be able to wake him up.

He dismounted and went to the front door. He thought about knocking, but if Sam Starr was in a drunken stupor, he wouldn't hear.

He opened the door and stepped in.

"Belle!" a man shouted from the other room. "Is that you?"

Sam Starr came staggering out of what was probably his and Belle's bedroom. He was naked and covered with sweat that had more than likely come out of a bottle and was working its way out of his pores. He stared at Clint.

"What the hell are you doin' here?" Starr roared. "Do you know where Belle is?"

"Yes, I do, Sam," Clint said. "You better get cleaned up and come with me."

"Why should I come with you?" Starr demanded.

"Because Belle needs you," Clint said. "She's been shot."

"What? Who shot her? You?"

"No, not me," Clint said. "Look, the doctor is trying to save her, and he sent me to get you. He said you better hurry, just in case."

"Just in case?"

73

Clint nodded.

"Gimme a minute," Starr said.

Chapter Eighteen

Starr and Clint rode hell-bent-for-leather back to town. Clint could have outdistanced him on Eclipse, but that wouldn't have served any purpose. It was Starr who had to get there before Belle died, not him.

When they got to town, there was still a small crowd in front of the doctor's office. They scattered as Clint and Starr rode up to them.

The two men dismounted and ran into the doctor's office. As they did, a man turned and faced them. It was Bass Reeves.

"What the hell are you doin' here?" Starr demanded.

"I heard Belle was shot," Reeves said. "I came to see if I could do anything."

"Like what? Arrest her?"

"I don't have any reason to arrest her or you right now, Starr. Who would you rather have here, Frank West?"

"Mr. Starr?" the doctor said, appearing at the doorway.

"Yeah, Doc?"

"You better come in and be with your wife."

Starr glared at Reeves, looked at Clint and then followed the doctor.

"Any idea how she is?" Clint asked the deputy.

"The doc says he got the bullet out. It missed her heart, but did some damage. He won't know much more until . . . well, if she survives."

"So we just wait?"

"Seems like that's all there is to do."

"Except go and find out who shot her," Clint said.

"I'm a manhunter, Clint," Reeves said. "not a detective. I have to be told who did it, and then I'll go out and get them."

"Well then, I guess that leaves it up to me," Clint said.

Clint turned and headed for the door.

"Wait!"

He turned, looked at the big black man.

"I'm not doin' anybody any good here," Reeves said. "I might as well come with you and watch your back, maybe keep you from gettin' shot by the same shooter."

"Come on, then," Clint said.

They stepped outside the office, where there was still a scattered crowd, and the buckboard. There was blood soaked into the back of it.

"Whose buckboard is this?" Clint shouted.

"Mine." A man stepped forward. He was dressed like a farmer, looked about fifty or so, slope-shouldered and deep-chested.

"Where did you find her?"

"Just off the road," the man said. "Actually, my horse must've smelled her blood, and he went a little crazy, so I stopped. I found her lyin' there, her shirt soaked with it, so I picked her up, put her in the buckboard and high-tailed it to town."

"Can you take me to where you found her?"

"Sure, Mister, but why?"

"We're gonna try to find out who shot 'er," Bass Reeves said.

The man noticed the badge on Reeves' chest, and said, "Well, okay, Deputy. Can I, uh, take the buck-board?"

Clint pointed to Sam Starr's horse.

"No, ride that."

"Uh, steal Sam Starr's horse?" the man asked, shocked. "I don't wanna get killed."

"What's your name?"

"David Williams," he said. "Folks call me Dave."

"Okay, Dave," Clint said, "I'm Clint Adams. You won't be stealing Starr's horse, you're borrowing it. And you're doing it to help us find out who shot his wife."

"Well, okay," Williams said, "As long as you tell 'im that."

"I will."

Clint looked at Reeves.

"Where's your horse?"

"Just down the street."

"Well you better get it," Clint said, "and let's ride."

***

Dave Williams led Clint and Bass Reeves out to the place where he had found Belle Starr lying. They dismounted, and Williams walked them off the road.

"There," he said, pointing to a bloody patch. "That's where I found her."

"She must've left the road here to ride to her house," Clint said to Reeves.

"So she must've been shot from the front." Reeves pointed. "That way."

"I thought you said you weren't a detective?" Clint asked.

"It's just common sense."

Clint looked at Williams.

"Stay with the horses."

"Right."

He looked at Reeves and said, "Come on, let's take a look around."

Chapter Nineteen

Clint and Reeves walked the area, checking the ground for any sign that someone had been there, waiting. Finally, Clint saw the remnants of a cigarette.

"There, see it?" he said, pointing.

"I see it." Reeves walked over. "And boot prints, here."

Clint walked over. A spent cigarette, and the boot prints of one man.

"She was shot twice, by two different shooters," he told Reeves. "Let's find where the other was waiting."

"Right."

They split up to keep searching and then Reeves shouted, "Here!"

Clint joined him, saw the boot prints on the ground. The two shooters had been about twenty feet apart.

"Two pros," Clint said. "They made sure there was daylight between them."

"And they picked up after themselves," Reeves said. "No spent shells."

"So somebody sent two pros after Belle," Clint said. "Let's find where these two left their horses."

They kept walking away from the road, started travelling in widening circles until Clint found the hoof prints they were looking for.

"Over here!" he shouted.

Reeves joined him, and they studied the ground together. Clint mentally bowed to the marshal's superior tracking skills.

"Well," he asked, "what do you see?"

"Two horses," Reeves said, "one tracks deeper than the others, so one of them was much larger and heavier."

"Looks like we need to find two men riding different size horses," Clint said.

"Not only that," Reeves said, "from their strides I'd say one man was tall and the other short."

"That's good," Clint said. "They should stand out."

They both stood.

"Can we track them from here?" Clint asked.

"We can try," Reeves said. "If, as you say, they're professionals, they're gonna do somethin' to cover their tracks somewhere along the way."

"Well," Clint suggested, "let's try tracking them until that happens, and then we'll see where we are."

"What about this fella, Williams?" Reeves asked, jerking his head to indicate the man holding their horses.

"I don't think he had anything to do with it," Clint said. "Let's cut him loose."

"Agreed."

They walked back to where Williams stood with the horses.

"You're free to go," Clint said.

"I am?"

"Yes."

"Thank God," he said. "All I did was find a body. I thought you were gonna accuse me of . . . somethin'."

"We're not accusing you of anything," Clint said. "Except trying to help. Thanks. Just take Sam Starr's horse back to town and grab your buckboard."

"Thanks, Mister," Williams said.

"No," Clint said, "thank you."

As Williams rode away, Clint turned to Reeves and asked, "Are you ready?"

"I'm always ready to track some villains," Reeves said.

"Then let's go."

They mounted up and rode off.

***

"It ends here," Reeves said.

"What?"

"They've covered their tracks from here on. And up ahead the terrain turned hard, almost rock like. Won't be able to pick up any tracks from there."

"So what if we just kept riding? Eventually, they'd come to softer ground."

"That could take days," Reeves said. "I could do that, but are you willing?"

"Not really," Clint said. "I want to get back to town, see how Belle's doing."

"Okay, then," Reeves said, "you do that, and I'll keep ridin'. Like you say, if we come to some soft ground, I might pick up the trail, again."

"All right," Clint said, "but if you catch up to them, bring them back here, not to Fort Smith. I want to talk to them before Judge Parker strings them up."

"I don't know that he'd do that," Reeves said.

"Why not? They tried to kill somebody," Clint said. "He's hung men for less."

"That's true," Bass Reeves said, "but in this case the person they tried to kill was . . . well, after all . . . Belle Starr."

"So?"

"The Outlaw Queen?" Reeves said. "The Judge might take that into account."

"Let's cross that bridge when we come to it," Clint said. "I'll see you back in Eufaula."

Chapter Twenty

When Clint got back to Eufaula, he immediately went to Dr. Hewitt's office to check on Belle Starr.

He entered the office, found Sam Starr sitting in the outer office.

"What's going on?" Clint asked.

Starr looked up at him.

"There was, uh, an emergency, the doctor said. He had to operate on Belle."

"And? Is she okay?"

"For now. Where's Reeves?"

"We found some tracks near where Belle was shot," Clint said. "Bass is tracking them."

"The shooters?"

Clint nodded.

"There were apparently two of them."

"And if he catches them, he'll take 'em to Fort Smith?" Starr asked.

"No, he agreed to bring them here," Clint said. "I want to question them."

Starr stood up.

"Why are you really here?" he asked.

"Sit back down, Sam, and I'll tell you."

They both sat.

"Belle contacted Roxy Doyle to ask for her help. Roxy couldn't come, so she asked me to. It's that simple."

"There ain't nothin' simple about this," Starr said. "You get here to help Belle with . . . what? And then she gets shot."

"That may be what she wanted the help with," Clint said. "She told me someone was coming here to kill her."

"Who?"

"Apparently someone from the prison in Detroit."

"Why didn't she tell me?" Starr asked.

"She said you were too concerned about yourself," Clint said. "That you wouldn't listen. She said you were drinking and . . . and whoring."

Starr put his head in his hands for a moment, then looked at Clint again.

"She's right," he said. "I was doin' that. I'm so sorry."

"You'll have to tell her that."

"If she lives," Starr said.

"Look," Clint said, "this all happened too fast, and I wasn't able to stop it. But maybe we can find out who did it and keep it from happening again."

"Ain't that what Reeves is doin'?"

"Bass is trying to catch up to the actual shooters," Clint said. "I think they were sent here by someone. And that person could always send others."

"Do you think that person is here? In town?"

Clint shrugged.

"I don't know," he said. "They could still be in prison in Detroit. But they have to be communicating through someone."

"There's no telegraph here," Starr said. "They'd have to go to Fort Smith for that."

"Okay," Clint said, "so maybe they're in Fort Smith."

"Then what are we waiting for?" Starr asked. "Let's go."

"I think I should go to Fort Smith," Clint said. "Reeves is out there hunting down the shooters. Somebody has to be here to protect Belle. Especially since she can't exactly protect herself, right now."

"Ya got a point," Starr said. "Besides, I don't wanna be away if she . . ."

"I know," Clint said. "So you stay, I'll go."

"When?"

"First thing in the morning," Clint said. "My horse needs to rest tonight."

"I'll stay in town, in a hotel," Starr said. "I want to be close by, and the doc won't let me sleep here."

"Do you have anybody who can watch your back?" Clint asked. "I mean, just in case."

"I know some people," Starr said. "In fact, I can use them to help protect Belle. We can make sure somebody's here at all times."

"That sounds like a good idea."

At that point the doctor came out, drying his hands on a white towel that was stained with blood.

"There was some internal bleeding," he told them. "I've stopped it, for now."

"Is she gonna make it?" Starr asked.

"I think if she lives through the next forty-eight hours, or so, she should be all right. I'll just have to watch her until then."

"Okay, Doc," Clint said. "Starr's going to stay around while I try to find out who did this to her, keep it from happening again."

"That sounds like a good idea," Doc Hewitt said. "I'd hate to have all my hard work go to waste."

"We'll do our best to try to see that doesn't happen," Clint promised.

Chapter Twenty-One

The oddest thing to happen to Clint in a long time was the fact that he was now working with Bass Reeves and Sam Starr. Roxy Doyle had better appreciate what he was doing, when she heard about it.

He had an early breakfast the next morning, checked in with Doc Hewitt about Belle's condition—no change—and confirmed that Sam Starr was sober and watching over Belle. Then he left town and headed for Fort Smith. It was an 80-mile ride, but because he was riding Eclipse, he arrived before dusk.

Fort Smith was bustling, bringing people in to shop at stores, eat in restaurants, even though it was best known for Judge Isaac Parker, his court, his prison, and his gallows. There were usually at least three nooses hanging at the ready, and Clint saw that there was no change as he rode in.

He got Eclipse situated at a livery, then himself at a hotel before stopping into a nearby restaurant for a meal. He wasn't surprised when a man wearing a badge entered, spotted him and approached while he was eating.

"Mr. Adams?"

"Yes, Deputy," Clint said.

"Judge Parker would like to see you in his chambers."

Judge Parker tended to know everything that was happening in town, sometimes before it even happened.

"Tell the judge I'll be along as soon as I've finished eating."

"Er, the Judge isn't usually in his chambers that late, sir," the man said. "He'd like you to come now, so he can go to supper."

Clint studied the man. He was a little young to be one of Parker's men, which was probably why the Judge had him delivering messages rather than riding out into Indian Territory.

"What's your name?"

"Uh. Gallagher, sir," the young man said, "Deputy Rob Gallagher."

"Well, Deputy Gallagher, I happen to be eating my supper right now," Clint said. "You tell the Judge I'll be along as soon as I finish. If he doesn't want to wait for me, that's up to him."

The deputy swallowed and said, "Uh, yes, sir. I'll tell 'im."

"And don't let him bite your head off," Clint said. "He can save that for me. After all, I'm the one making him wait."

"Yes, sir," the deputy said. "Thank you, sir."

The deputy left, and Clint went back to his steak.

***

When Clint got to Judge Parker's chambers, the judge's middle-aged clerk frowned at him over his wire-framed glasses.

"Adams?"

"That's right."

"He's in a foul mood."

"What else is new?"

"I'll tell him you're here."

"Thank you."

The clerk knocked on the judge's door and went in. Clint heard shouting, and then the clerk came out, looking shaken.

"Uh, you can go in."

"Did he bite your head off?"

"Oh, yes," the clerk said.

"My fault, I guess," Clint said. "Sorry."

The clerk waved.

"All in a day's work, sir."

Clint opened the judge's door without knocking and entered. It had been several years since he'd seen the man, and, if anything, his mutton chops had gotten thicker, and grayer.

Judge Isaac Parker frowned at Clint from behind his large, oak desk. There was a window right behind him, from where he usually watched the hangings.

"Your arrogance knows no bounds," Parker said to him.

"Nice to see you again, too, Judge." Clint sat in the chair across from Parker.

"I didn't invite you to sit."

Clint ignored the comment and stared at the man. The Judge always had it in for him, especially since he had turned down several offers to wear a deputy's badge.

"What are you doing in Fort Smith?" he asked.

"Bass Reeves told me you miss me."

Parker scowled.

"Where is Reeves?"

"Chasing some shooters through the Territories."

"Shooters?" Parker repeated. "What shooters? Who did they shoot?"

"Belle Starr."

"What?" Parker snapped. "Is she dead?"

"No."

"And Reeves is trying to find the men who killed her?"

"We both were, but we've split up."

"And you've come here. Why?"

"Because somebody sent those men to kill Belle Starr," Clint said. "Was it you?"

"I control marshals," Parker said, "not killers. But if someone did try to kill Belle Starr, I'm sorry they didn't succeed. And I'm sorry they didn't kill that husband of hers, too."

"Why didn't you?"

"What?"

"Why didn't you kill them when you had the chance?" Clint asked. "Hang them for their crimes?"

"Their crimes did not include murder," Parker said.

"That's never stopped you before."

"Despite what you think of me," Parker said, "I've never put anyone to death who didn't deserve it."

"That may be," Clint said, "but I'm not here about you. I came to find out who wants Belle Starr dead."

"Who doesn't?"

"But who wants it badly enough to take action," Clint said.

"I can't tell you that, because I don't know."

"I never thought you did."

"Then why are you here?"

"Well, I'm here in your chambers because you sent for me," Clint said. "Otherwise I'd be out there trying to find the killer."

"Then get out of here," Parker said, "and do that. And then get out of Fort Smith."

Clint stood up and said, "As soon as I can."

Chapter Twenty-Two

Clint left Parker's building, with no intention of ever going back there. What he needed was to know if anyone had sent telegrams to Fort Smith concerning Belle Starr—possibly from as far away as Detroit.

The hotel he was staying at was called The Marlboro Hotel. He entered the lobby and approached the front desk.

"Is there something I can help you with, sir?" the clerk asked.

"Yes," Clint said, "how many telegraph offices are there in Fort Smith?"

"Several," the man said. "I can direct you to the nearest one."

"I need to know where they all are," Clint said.

"I'll write that information down for you."

The clerk did so, and handed the slip of paper to Clint.

"Thank you."

When Clint turned from the desk to go to his room, he saw someone enter the hotel wearing one of Judge Parker's badges.

"Who's that?" he asked the clerk.

"That's Deputy Marshal Magnus," the clerk said.

"Magnus?" Clint repeated. "I don't know the name."

As the woman walked toward him the clerk said, "Judge Parker's only female deputy marshal."

***

Deputy Marshal Magnus and Clint entered the Marlboro Saloon through the lobby entrance.

"We need to talk," she had said to him, without preamble.

"Where?" he asked.

"Next door," she said. "The saloon. It's maintained for guests here, and is never very busy."

He could see as soon as they entered that she was right. There were only a couple of men in there, drinking. The bartender looked bored, but brightened when he saw them.

"Deputy Magnus," he said. "Haven't seen you in a while."

"Two beers, Grady."

"Comin' up."

He set the beers on the bar. Magnus picked them both up and led Clint to a table. They sat across from each other and she pushed one over to him.

"How the hell did you get Judge Parker to appoint you?" Clint asked. "This is not the sort of thing one would ever expect him to do."

"It wasn't easy," she said. "I had to prove my worth."

She was a tall woman, very fit, with long black hair shot with gray, and a scar that pretty much bisected her face. It started at her forehead, went down between her eyes and across her nose, making it look slightly crooked. It stopped just shy of her upper lip. And it was somewhat red, indicating it was still fairly new.

"Yes," she said, "that's how I got the scar. With my face almost cut in half, he couldn't very well refuse me."

"Can I ask how—"

"Perhaps I'll tell you another time," she said. "Right now, I need to ask you something."

"All right, go ahead."

"Why the hell are you acting on behalf of Belle Starr?"

"I'm actually not," he said. "I'm acting on behalf of Roxy Doyle."

"Lady Gunsmith?"

"That's right."

"Why her?"

"She's friends with Belle," Clint said, "and she asked me to help."

"And you agreed?" Magnus asked. "Knowing who Belle Starr is?"

"No, I agreed," Clint replied, "knowing who Roxy Doyle is."

Chapter Twenty-Three

"Why are you here?" Clint asked. "Why seek me out?"

"I've heard talk about you," she said. "From Judge Parker, from Bass Reeves, from other deputies."

"And?"

"They all say you're a man to be trusted."

"Even Parker?"

She grinned.

"He doesn't say many good things about you, but he does say that. It still stings him that you turned down a badge."

"I'm wondering how you got one."

"Like I said," she replied, touching her face, "it wasn't easy, but I managed to impress him."

"So what do you want from me?"

"I managed to get him to give me a badge, but I'm at a standstill. He won't send me out. But if I go with you, and we find out who tried to kill Belle Starr—"

"How'd you know about that?"

"Parker's clerk," she said. "He tells me things."

"Why?" Clint asked. "Isn't he loyal to the Judge?"

"He is," she said, "but he wants to sleep with me."

"Really?"

She sat back.

"Is that so hard to believe?"

It actually wasn't. She had a good body under the trail clothes she was wearing, and other than the scar on her face, she was attractive.

"No," Clint said, "not at all—from your end. He just doesn't strike me as the type."

"Oh. Well, okay then," she said. "Let me work with you. I can help."

"How?"

"There are some things a woman can do that a man can't," she pointed out. "Places she can go that he can't."

"You might be right. But to start with, let's do something we can both do."

"Like what?"

"I need to check all the telegraph offices in Fort Smith for telegrams that they received in the past week."

"Saying what?" she asked.

"Something that could be read as instructions to kill Belle Starr," Clint said.

"You mean like . . . in code?"

"Well," he said, "not in plain English, let's put it that way. Nothing is going to say 'kill Belle Starr.'"

"I get it."

"I've got a list of six locations," Clint said. "That's a lot for a town this size."

"Well," Magnus said, "there are three thousand people livin' here, now."

"That's a lot, about the same size as Kansas City."

"A couple of these are private. Rich men buy what they want, don't they?"

"That they do," Clint said. "You take those."

"Why me?"

"Well, one, you're from here, and two, I hate rich men. Just flash your badge and ask your questions."

"Okay."

"You want to copy down these addresses?"

"I'll remember. We start first thing in the mornin'?"

"I'd start tonight, but I'm sure the offices are closed, and the rich men are . . . out."

"I'll hit them early tomorrow. Where and when do you want to meet so we can exchange information?"

"Let's make it lunch," he said. "You pick the place."

"Vito's," she said. "It's an Italian restaurant on Loyola Street. One O'clock?"

"I'll be there."

"Thanks for this, Mr. Adams."

"Call me Clint, since we're working together."

"I'm Helen."

They shook hands across the table, and then she stood up.

"One o'clock," she said again, and left.

Clint picked up the rest of his beer and walked back to the bar.

"Cold one?" the man asked.

"Sure."

"That's one hard woman," he said, putting the beer in front of Clint.

"Is she?"

"She probably wanted somethin', if she was all sweetness and light to you."

"Not exactly, but you might be right," Clint said. "She didn't play it hard."

"You a lawman, too?"

"No."

"Well, I'd watch it with her," the bartender said. "They say that scar on her face has affected more than just her looks."

"Her mind, you mean?"

The bartender nodded.

"She's killed some people who didn't deserve it," the man said. "She does that when she loses her temper."

"Well," Clint said, "I guess I'm going to have to make sure I don't give her a reason to lose her temper."

Chapter Twenty-Four

The next morning Clint had a quick breakfast, nothing heavy, since he was having an Italian lunch with Deputy Marshal Helen Magnus. Afterward, he hit the three telegraph offices. Since he had no badge to flash, he had to do some quick talking to get the clerks to show him their files.

But there was nothing, no messages that could be interpreted as kill orders. When he reached Vito's on Loyola Street, he wasn't in a good mood, and hoped that Marshal Magnus had better news.

He waited for her outside and, after fifteen minutes she came walking up to him.

"Anything?" he asked.

"Maybe," she said. "Let's go inside."

They entered and a tuxedoed maître d' greeted Magnus by name.

"Deputy Magnus, how nice. Joining us for lunch?"

"Yes, Tony. And this is my friend, Clint Adams."

"Mr. Adams, welcome to Vito's. Right this way. Your regular table is waiting, Deputy."

He led them to a table that was not only in the back, but in an alcove, so that there was privacy.

"Wow," Clint said, "how do you rate treatment like this?"

"It helps to be rich."

"What?" he said. "Wait, you're rich?"

"I am," she said. "I have a big house here in Fort Smith."

"Why didn't you tell me that last night?"

"I was going to, but you had just finished telling me how you hated rich people."

"Men," he corrected her, "I said I hate rich men."

"Ah, I should have recognized the distinction."

"So, if you're rich, why do you want to be one of Judge Parker's deputies?"

"I was bored, mostly. And after my husband was murdered, I decided I should do something worthwhile."

"Murdered?" he asked. "I'm sorry."

"Oh, it was a long time ago. After that I got myself trained with a gun, studied the law and, when I was ready, approached Judge Parker. He knew my husband, which was probably one of the reasons he took me on."

"So now you're trying to prove to him that you deserve the badge."

"Definitely."

A waiter came by and Clint allowed Magnus to do the ordering.

"I hope you don't mind wine," she said.

"I prefer beer, but for this meal I'll make an exception."

The waiter brought them each a glass of red wine.

"So I came up empty," he said. "I hope you didn't."

"Two of the three telegraph lines were private. I happened to know the two men who had them installed in their homes. They both allowed me to see the telegrams that came to them in the past week or so. There was nothing like what we're looking for."

"And you believe them?"

"Yes," she said, "even though they're rich, I believe they told me the truth."

"And the third office?"

"Ah," she said, "now there I found something interesting."

"What?"

"A telegram that was sent to a man named Butler," she said.

"And what did it say?"

"I have a copy here."

She brought out a telegraph flimsy upon which was written the words: DO IT.

"This is it?"

"That's all."

"When did it come in?"

"Last week."

He put it down on the table and tapped it thoughtfully with his finger.

"I suppose it could mean a lot of things," he said.

"It could," she said. "But it's all we've got."

"And did the telegraph operator know this Butler? Or where he lives?"

"Not at all," she said. "He said the man came in, picked up the telegram, and left."

"Didn't he send a reply?"

"No."

"And where did the telegram come from?"

"Kansas City."

"From Kansas City to Fort Smith to Eufaula," Clint said.

"But where did it originate from?"

"I'm thinking Detroit," he said, "but we'd have to check with the office in Kansas City."

"We could send them a telegram and ask," Magnus recommended.

"We should do that after lunch," he said.

"Good," she said. "We'll eat and then I'll take you there."

"Helen, can I ask you something?"

"About the scar?"

"Yes."

"Go ahead." She sipped her wine.

"Did that come before or after Parker gave you a badge?"

"I got it after," she said. "While I was on an assignment. It was after this injury that he stopped sending me out."

"I guess he doesn't want you getting hurt again," he said. "Who knew Judge Parker had a heart?"

"Oh, he doesn't," she said. "He just doesn't want a woman getting killed on his watch."

Chapter Twenty-Five

When they finished their excellent meal and heaped praise on Tony and his chef, they left and headed for the telegraph office. When they arrived, the clerk remembered Magnus and asked if he could do anything else for "the deputy?"

"Yes," she said, "we'd like to track down the origin of this telegram.

"Well, it came from Kansas City," the clerk said. "Wasn't that what you wanted to know?"

"Yes, but now we want to know where Kansas City got it from? Can we send them a telegram asking?"

"Uh, sure, I guess," he said. "Do you wanna write it out?"

"You know what we want," Clint said. "Just ask the operator there where it came from."

"Okay."

"We'll be outside," Clint said.

There was a wooden bench right outside the door, so they sat on it, side-by-side.

Suddenly, Magnus moved, as if to put space between them.

"What's wrong?" Clint asked.

"Nothing, I—I just realized I could use a bath. I must stink."

"Of what?" he asked. "You smell fine."

"Sweat," she said, "I smell like sweat."

"Yeah, but it's woman sweat," Clint said. "That's the best kind."

She grinned at him and said, "You're crazy, you know that?"

"Why, because I like the way women smell?"

"I would think you'd want a woman with, you know, lilac water or something."

"No," he said, "I prefer women who smell like women. And you, you're definitely a woman."

Suddenly, she put her hand over her face.

"Now what?"

"You're complimenting me," she said, "and I'm suddenly very self-conscious about the scar. I wore it as a badge of courage until I met you—"

The clerk came out at that point.

"Here you go," he said. "The message originated from a telegraph office in Detroit, Michigan."

"That's it," Clint said. "Belle and Sam Starr were in prison there."

"Thank you," Magnus said to the clerk.

"Any time, Deputy."

He went back inside.

"Now what?" she asked Clint.

"We need to find this Butler."

***

There was no indication on the telegram, or at the telegraph office, who Butler was or where he came from. The clerk was able to give only a general description, which could have fit a lot of men.

"I can put the word out with some of my contacts and see if anyone knows him," Deputy Magnus offered.

"Why don't you do that?" Clint said. "And we might as well take a break and get some supper. Maybe you'll let me treat you, this time," he added, since she had picked up the check at the Italian lunch.

"Not a chance," she said. "In fact, I was thinking of taking you to my house for supper. You could relax there much more than in a restaurant."

"My hotel's pretty comfortable—"

"Nonsense," she said, "no hotel room is as comfortable as a home. I insist. We can keep tossing this problem back and forth, as well."

"Well, all right, then," he said. "But I need to go back to my hotel to clean up, so let me have your address."

"Good," she said, "that'll give me time to take a bath."

She gave him the address. They agreed on a time and then split up. She went home, and he went to his hotel.

***

Clint made one stop on the way to the hotel. It was at Judge Parker's building. Only he wasn't there to talk to Parker, but to his clerk.

The man looked up from his desk as Clint entered, and frowned.

"The Judge didn't send for you."

"I'm here to see you."

"Me?" The man sat up straight. "Why me?"

"What's your name?"

"Steve Davidson."

Clint suddenly realized that the little man reminded him of a rabid Chihuahua. No wonder Helen Magnus didn't want to sleep with him.

"Mr. Davidson, does the judge have a deputy marshal named Helen Magnus?"

"Why yes, he does," Davidson said. "Do you know Hel—uh, Deputy Magnus?"

"I met her recently," Clint said. "We're working together."

"I don't know if the Judge is going to like that," Davidson said.

"Well, he can take that up with his deputy when he sees her," Clint said. "I just wanted to check with you to make sure she was legitimate."

"Yes," Davidson said, "She's a legitimate deputy."

"And she's rich?"

"Oh yes," the man said. "Very."

"So she's been telling me the truth."

"Apparently."

"Okay," Clint said, "thanks."

"You don't want to see the judge?"

"As you said," Clint reminded him, "he didn't send for me."

He turned and left the office, and the building.

***

Back at his hotel he took a bath, dressed in some fresh clothes he had brought with him. Nothing fancy, just clean. Then he left the hotel, waved down a horse drawn cab and had it take him to the address Helen Magnus had given him for her house.

"That's a pretty fancy neighborhood," the driver said.

"So I've been told," Clint said, and sat back to enjoy the ride.

109

Chapter Twenty-Six

After Clint left the clerk's office the man rose, knocked on the judge's door and entered.

"What do you want, Davidson?" Parker asked, from his desk. "I didn't call you in."

"No, sir, but I thought you'd want to know that Clint Adams was just here."

"And you didn't let him in," Parker said. "Good man."

"He didn't want to come in, sir. He, uh, didn't come to see you."

"Who did he come to see, then?"

"Uh, me."

"What the hell did he want?"

"He wanted to know about Deputy Magnus."

"Jesus," Parker, said, running his face with his hands. Then he dropped them to his desktop and said to Davidson, "You'd better sit down and tell me about it."

***

Clint saw what the driver meant when they entered the area. All of the homes were large, two story buildings, some of which looked as if they had been built very recently. When the cab pulled to a stop in front of Magnus' house, he realized hers was one of the fanciest.

He paid the driver and walked up the path to the front door. Of the wealthy women he had met in the past, he liked most of them. They didn't seem to have the same arrogance as wealthy men. That was probably because the men usually wanted to take over and be in control. The women simply wanted to control their own lives.

When he knocked, she opened the door herself, wearing a beautiful blue dress, with her clean hair hanging in shimmering waves to her shoulders.

"Welcome," she said.

"I didn't expect you to answer the door yourself."

"Oh, I have servants," she said. "I gave them the night off."

"I see."

"Follow me, please."

She led him to a small, well-appointed room with a beautiful sofa and matching chairs.

"This is my sitting room," she said. "Would you like a brandy, or shall I just get you a beer?"

"I'll take the brandy," he said.

She walked to a sideboard and poured from a crystal decanter, then handed him a glass.

"Dinner is almost ready."

"You cooked?"

"That surprises you?"

"Most law officers I know who cook do it very badly," he said.

"I'm a very good cook," she said. "You'll see." She sipped her brandy, then put the glass down. "In fact, let me check on things. You can wait here. Make yourself comfortable."

As she left, he looked around at the bookshelves that encircled the room. There were many books by authors he had read—Twain, Dickens, Robert Louis Stevenson, Jules Verne, Sir Walter Scott. There were also many by authors he had never heard of.

After circling the room, he settled on the sofa and breathed in the aromas that were coming from the kitchen.

In moments, Helen Magnus reappeared. She reclaimed her drink, and sat across form him, in an armchair that seemed to fit her very well. He was willing to bet she spent a lot of time in that chair.

"So," she said, "did you check up on me?"

"I did," Clint said.

"I thought you might," she said. "After all, who would believe a rich woman would want to be a deputy marshal in Judge Parker's court? Did you talk to Parker?"

"No, Davidson."

"Him? What did he have to say?"

"Just that you were legitimately a deputy marshal."

"And you didn't talk to Parker?"

"Not if I don't have to."

"But you know Davidson's going to tell Parker you were there."

"Probably."

"Well," she said, "the judge will probably bitch about it. The only question is, will he bitch at me, or you?"

"I guess we'll find out," Clint said.

"Well then," she said, "let's go have dinner. We can discuss our options while we eat."

"Our options?"

"Yes," she said as they walked through the house, "what our next move should be."

"As I see it, we've only got one move," Clint said. "Finding Butler."

"Yes, but how are we going to do that?" she asked. "And do we look for him here, or in Eufaula?"

"That is a good question."

Chapter Twenty-Seven

Magnus had prepared a roast chicken dinner, complete with vegetables and biscuits. It was as good as any Clint had in a restaurant.

While they ate, they discussed finding Butler, who was either the man who shot Belle Starr, or the man who hired someone to shoot her.

"The telegram apparently tells him to get it done," Clint said. "No indication whether or not he's to do it himself."

"Do you know a gunman named Butler?" she asked.

"No," he said. The only Butler he'd even known had been his friend, James Butler "Wild Bill" Hickok.

"I don't, either," she said. "At least, not here in the territories."

"It might make sense," he said, "for us to split up. You keep checking here in Fort Smith, and I'll go back to Eufaula. If this Butler hired it done, he might be back here. If he did it himself, he might be staying in Eufaula to finish the job, if he has to."

"You mean, if Belle Starr is still alive."

"Yes," Clint said. "She was when I left. I can only hope she still is."

"Is she a friend?"

"More the friend of a friend," he said.

"So there's nothing . . . between you?"

"Me and Belle Starr? No."

He wondered why she asked that? Was she interested in him? Was that the reason for this dinner at her house? So far there had been no indication of interest—unless, of course, it was the dress, her hair, and the fresh from the bath smell of her. He noticed she hadn't doused herself with anything resembling lilac water.

"Dessert?" she asked. "Or are you too full?"

"Never too full for dessert," he said.

"That's good," she said. "I made a chocolate cake."

"You made it?"

"Yes," she said, "I can both cook and bake." She stood up. "I'm multi-talented, which you will soon see."

Now that was a remark that could have been construed as suggestive.

"With coffee?" she asked.

"Yes, please."

"Comin' up." She picked up some plates to take to the kitchen with her.

"Can I help?"

"No, no," she said, "you're my guest. You just stay where you are."

He heard her moving around in the kitchen, and then she reappeared carrying a tray with a cake, plates, a pot of coffee and cups on it.

"By multi-talented do you mean you were once a waitress?" he asked.

"Nope," she said, "never had that job. I'm just strong, and good at balancing things."

She put the tray down on the table, then cut the cake and handed him a piece. She followed that by pouring coffee and setting a cup in front of him. It smelled and looked good and strong.

She sat down and did the same for herself, then said, "Dig in."

He took a bite and found it very nearly the best chocolate cake he'd ever had.

"Wow," he said.

"I told you," she said. "I can bake."

"And make coffee," he said, after a sip. "What can't you do?"

"There's nothing I can't do, Clint Adams," she said. "You're going to find that out."

Chapter Twenty-Eight

After dinner and dessert, Helen Magnus led the way back to her sitting room and poured more brandy. They sat as they had before, Clint still wondering what—if anything—the rest of the evening held.

"Has Judge Parker ever been here?" he asked.

"He has," she said, "when my husband was still alive."

"Not since?"

"No," she said, "the Judge and I don't socialize. I work for him, just like Bass Reeves and the others."

"But your husband was his friend."

"Right," she said, "they were friends. I've never been friends with Parker. And I likely never will."

"You know," Clint said, "I always had the feeling Judge Parker didn't approve of women. Especially since he's hanged one or two."

"You're probably right," she said. "He's barely civil to me."

"And yet he gave you a badge."

"Well," she said, looking sheepish, "I may have forced his hand, there."

Clint stared at her.

"You have something on Judge Parker, don't you, Helen?" he asked.

She didn't answer, but adopted the look of the cat who caught the canary.

"What is it?"

"I can't say."

"So you *do* have something on him."

"I never said that!"

"You didn't deny it," he said. "You know something about him, probably something you heard from your husband. And you promised never to reveal it."

"I made that promise to my husband," she said. "Not the Judge."

Clint fell silent a moment. As much as he would have liked to know what she had on the Judge, he wasn't going to ask her to break her promise to her dead husband. That wouldn't have been fair to her.

"Okay," he said, "I guess I'll just have to be satisfied to know that there *is* something about Judge Parker that he doesn't want people to know."

"And now," she said, moving from her armchair to sit beside him on the sofa, "let's talk about something other than business."

"What did you have in mind?"

"Oh," she said, taking his glass from him and setting it aside, "I think you know what I have in mind."

She moved even closer to him, filling his nostrils with her scent—the scent of a woman. But he hesitated just a second when she leaned in, and she drew back, looking puzzled at first, and then afraid.

"What is it?" she asked. "Is it the scar?" She moved her hand to her face.

"No," he said, pushing her hand away, "I think it's the badge."

"But . . . I don't have it on."

"Judge Parker's deputies always have the badge on," Clint said.

"Listen," she said, "I may be as tough as any of his other deputies, but I'm also a woman. You said so yourself."

"You're right," he said, touching her arm, "you smell like a woman, you feel like a woman, and I'm sure you're going to taste like a woman."

"Then why don't you taste and find out?" she asked.

He drew her to him, then, and kissed her. He was right, she tasted just like a woman. Her mouth was hot and avid, and tasted sweet.

He pushed her so that she was lying on her back on the sofa, and he began to undo the buttons and stays on her dress. When he had the top open, full breasts bloomed into view, their dark nipples already distended with passion. He kissed her breasts, sucked on her nipples,

119

until she was struggling to get the dress off the rest of the way.

She lifted her hips and he pulled the dress down and away. Now she was fully naked on the sofa, and the forest of hair between her legs—as dark as the hair on her head—was calling to him.

"Wait," she said, as he knelt next to the sofa. "You have too many clothes on, and too much gun."

He removed the gunbelt and set it on the table in front of the sofa, where it would come quickly to hand if he needed it. Then he stood and undressed while her eyes watched his every move and widened as more and more of his skin came into view. Then, when his hard penis was free, she reached for it, taking it into her hand.

"My husband was much older than I was," she said. "we had sex very little to begin with, and hardly at all near the end. But he never had a penis like this, so hard and beautiful."

But Helen Magnus was at least forty, and she had sex before she married her older husband, so while she may have been out of practice, she was by no means inexperienced.

And she proceeded to prove that . . .

***

It didn't take that long to eat dinner.

Steve Davidson stood in an alley between two houses across the street, his eyes on Helen Magnus' house. It was all lit up, but there was no light upstairs, where the bedroom was. That was the only solace he felt.

Once he knew that Clint Adams and Helen Magnus had met, he'd felt sure they would end up at her house. That was why he took up position across the street before they even arrived. Once they did arrive and go inside, he settled in to wait. He was hoping she would give him dinner, and then he would leave.

That didn't appear to be the case.

Certainly enough time to eat and leave had gone by. So they must have been doing something else, and knowing the Gunsmith's reputation with women, he knew what that had to be.

And he knew Helen Magnus was a sexual animal. He'd known that since the day he met her. After so many years living with an older man, and now a few years with no man at all, he knew she wouldn't be able to resist the advances of a man like Clint Adams.

Damn him!

Chapter Twenty-Nine

Helen Magnus got off the sofa, stood in front of Clint and put her hands on him. She stroked the flesh of his chest, his belly, slid her hands up his naked back, pulled him close and kissed him. The scar on her face meant nothing. Her lips were sweet, her breath was hot, her tongue was alive in his mouth. He slid his arms around her, ran his palms over her smooth, hot skin, down so he could cup her buttocks in his hands and pull her closer. Her breasts were full and firm between them, her nipples making little dents in his chest.

She moaned into his mouth, slid one hand between them so she could grasp his cock. He knew there had to be a bed somewhere in that house, but they were doing just fine where they were.

She broke the kiss so she could run her mouth over his neck, his shoulders, his chest, down over his belly, and then she went to her knees so she could go lower. She kissed his thighs, then pressed her face to his hard cock. She licked it, up and down, top and underside, and when she had it good and wet, she gripped his ass in her hands and pulled him into her mouth.

She began to move her head back and forth, letting her lips glide over the smooth surface of his cock. After doing that for a while, she released him, looked up and said, "Lie down on the sofa."

"Shouldn't we find a bed?" he asked.

"I'm too impatient," she said, getting to her feet. "Lie down."

He got on the sofa, lying on his back, and she knelt next to it. She spent some more time sucking him, and then stood, mounted him, and took him inside. Her heat closed around his cock, bringing him intense pleasure, and then she started to move, increasing that pleasure.

"Oh, God," she moaned, riding him up and down, supporting herself with one hand on the back of the sofa, and the other pressed to his abdomen.

When waves of pleasure began to course through her body, she started to bounce on him uncontrollably. He reached for her hips, held them while she continued to move, and then she suddenly came down on him and stayed there. Her eyes went wide and she began to twist side-to-side, and suddenly he erupted inside of her, and they both yelled . . .

***

"I'm glad you sent the servants away," he said, a little later.

She was lying on top of him, her head on his chest, his cock still inside her and, remarkably, still almost fully hard.

"You're still hard inside me," she said.

"I noticed that," he said, sliding his hand up and down her back. "I think that has more to do with you then it does me."

"Don't be so sure," she said. "You may just be a re-markable man."

"Oh, I am," he said, "in many ways. For instance, without even looking, I'm sure there are beds in this place."

"Several," she said.

"Well," he said, "what do you say you show me one of them."

"I can do that," she said. "Would it be okay with you if we took a decanter of brandy with us?"

"Oh, I insist on it."

She started to move, then gasped and stopped.

"I don't really want you out of me," she said. "Not while you're still this hard."

"Then we have two choices," he said. "One, we can try to walk while still connected."

"Or?" she asked.

"Or you better start moving again."

She smiled.

"Oh, I can do that!"

She sat up and started riding him up and down, slowly at first, then faster and faster.

"Keep going," he said, "that's it, keep it up, faster, faster . . . oh boy, here it comes . . ."

***

Once he had exploded into her again, she eased him out of her and stood up.

"Wow," she said. "Still hard."

"Not fully," he said, getting to his feet. "Whew, my legs are weak."

"So are mine," she said. "And yet I feel so . . . alive. We should be tired."

"I agree."

"I'll get the brandy," she said.

She walked across the room to the sideboard, while he watched. He couldn't take his eyes off her naked form. Once she grabbed the decanter and two glasses, she said to him, "Follow me."

As she walked from the room, her butt twitching enticingly, he said, "My pleasure," grabbed his gunbelt, slung it over his shoulder, and followed.

Chapter Thirty

They spent time in her bed, consuming the brandy and each other. Once the brandy was gone, they fell asleep.

When Clint woke the next morning, he looked around to make sure his gun was nearby and saw, with satisfaction, that it was. Then he looked at the naked woman lying next to him on her belly and got the same satisfaction. He didn't give any thought to the apparent fact he got the same satisfaction from guns that he did from women. That would be for another time.

He reached over and slid the idle finger of his right hand along the clef between her buttocks.

"I know," she said, into the pillow, "you want breakfast."

"I was actually thinking of something else," he said, "but breakfast would do."

She slapped his hand away and rolled over.

"If I don't get up and make breakfast now, it might turn into lunch. Besides, I'm still worn out from last night." She looked at his limp cock. "Thankfully, you appear to be, too."

"I don't believe I've ever been that hard for that long, before."

"I'll take that as a compliment."

"I think it might have been the food," he added.

She slapped him on the arm and got off the bed. Grabbing a robe and wrapping it around her she said, "Give me half an hour, and then come down for breakfast." She pointed to a door. "You can wash up in there."

***

When he got downstairs, the diningroom table was covered with food. There were eggs, bacon, spuds and biscuits. When she came out of the kitchen with the coffee pot and two cups, he could see that she had also washed up and combed her lustrous hair. For the first time since the previous afternoon, he noticed the scar on her face, but only because it was so red.

"Hungry?" she asked.

"Famished."

"Well, sit down and start eating."

They both sat, she at the head of the table and he to her right, leaving the rest of the long expanse of table empty.

"When do your servants come back?"

"Tonight," she said, "unless I send them away again."

"I don't know if I'll be here tonight."

"Ah," she said, "our plan."

"Yes."

127

"Divide and conquer."

"Hopefully."

"What if the judge decides to send me out on an assignment?" she asked.

"What are the chances he'll do that?"

"Ordinarily, I'd say none, but things have changed."

"How?"

"By now he knows I'm working with you," she said. "He might want to ruin that and separate us."

"Just to be ornery," Clint added. "Yeah, I can see Parker doing that."

"I'll try to make sure he doesn't," she said.

"Blackmail?"

"No, no," she said, "I don't hold that over his head. Once was enough. No, I'll just make him see the sense in what we're doing."

"Finding the man who shot Belle Starr."

"Yes."

"I don't know that he'll ever see the sense to that."

"Well," she said, "let's just wait and see how persuasive I can be."

"I think," Clint said, "I already know the answer to that."

Chapter Thirty-One

After breakfast Clint and Magnus resisted the lure of the bedroom again. They each got dressed and met at the front door, wearing their guns and trail clothes. Once again Magnus looked like a deputy marshal.

"Deputy," he greeted.

"Mr. Gunsmith."

"Time for us to go," he said.

"I'll check in with my contacts, keep searching for this Butler, until Judge Parker calls me in. Then we'll see."

"And I'll go back to Eufaula," Clint said, "and look for him there."

"How do we stay in touch?" she asked.

"Do you know anyone who could act as a messenger between us?"

"I think I do," she said. "With a fast horse—"

"Not a fast one," Clint said. "Just make sure he has a good one."

"Right," she said, "one with stamina rather than speed."

"Exactly."

"My driver is back," she said, "and the buggy is waiting outside to take us back to town."

"Good," Clint said. "Then I'll collect my horse from the livery and get going."

They left the building and walked up the path to the buggy. The driver, a man in his fifties, stepped down from the driver's seat.

"Ma'am," he said. "Sir."

"Clint, this is Jacob, my driver."

"Jacob."

They climbed into the back. Jacob got into the driver's seat and drove them back to the center of town.

***

The driver left them in front of Judge Parker's building, which housed his office, his court, and the prison. Also, a barracks for his marshals—the ones who didn't have their own homes.

"Go home, Jacob," Magnus said. "I'll see you there."

"Yes, Ma'am. Sir."

Clint nodded. The man climbed aboard the buggy and drove off.

"I think I'm going to have to go in and report to the judge," she said.

"Then I'll say goodbye here, for now," Clint said. "If Parker stops you from doing what we agreed—"

"He won't," Magnus said. "I swear."

"If he orders you—"

"I'll disobey," she said. "And if he pushed it further, I'll resign."

"No, I don't want that," Clint said. "You waited so long to become a deputy. Don't give it up for this. One way or another, I'll find out who shot Belle Starr."

"Let's see what happens," she said, promising nothing.

He watched as she walked into the building, then turned and headed for the livery.

***

Steve Davidson looked up from his desk as Deputy Marshal Helen Magnus approached his desk.

"The Judge has been waiting for you," he said.

"For me to report in?"

"Not quite," Davidson said, stiffly. "Wait here."

Something was going on. She was tempted to leave but decided to find out what it was. Davidson returned from the Judge's chambers.

"You can go in."

"Thanks, Steve."

It was the first time she had ever called him by his first name.

As she entered Parker's chambers, he stood and said, "Just what the hell are you playing at, Deputy?"

"Sir?"

"Don't play dumb with me," he said. "You're working with Clint Adams."

"I'm doing my job, sir," she said.

"By trying to find out who shot Belle Starr?"

"Yes, sir."

"Who cares?"

"The law does," she said. "Or am I wrong, Judge? It's against the law to try to kill someone."

Parker looked annoyed.

"Technically, yes, but—"

"How else am I supposed to do my job but technically, sir?" she asked. "According to the law, and your rules."

"*My* rules?"

"Yes, sir," she said, "anyone who breaks the law must be punished. Isn't that your rule?"

Parker sat back in his chair and winced at the bad taste in his mouth of his own words being tossed back at him.

"Get out, Deputy," he said.

Chapter Thirty-Two

Clint rode back into Eufaula just after dark. It was peacefully quiet, with piano music emanating from one saloon and wafting down the street on a breeze.

He got to the livery just as the hostler was closing the doors.

"You're back," the man exclaimed happily. He opened the doors wide for Clint to ride Eclipse in. "How's our boy?"

"He's probably a little tired," Clint said. "I pushed him a bit, this time."

Clint dismounted, handed the reins to the man, then removed his saddlebags and rifle.

"That's okay," the hostler said, "I'll take good care of him."

"I know you will. Any news in town?"

"News? Oh, you mean like Belle Starr dying?"

"Did she?"

"Nossir, she didn't. Still hangin' on, they say."

"And Sam?"

"Looks like he ain't left her side."

"Okay, thanks."

"Same hotel?" the man called as Clint went out the door.

"Why not?"

***

He not only went to the same hotel, but got the same room. He dropped off his saddlebags and rifle, then went in search of a meal and a beer. He would have gone to Doc Hewitt's to check on Belle Starr, but it was late, and the doctor's office was probably locked up. There was really no reason for him to go pounding on the door. According to the hostler, she was still alive, so he could check in the morning.

He found a small restaurant, rather than go to one of the larger ones, figuring they'd be less busy after dark.

He got a table in the back—rarely a problem, since most people liked to sit in the open—and ordered a steak dinner and a beer.

After he finished eating, he went to the Last Race Saloon, elbowed himself a space at the crowded bar, and waved at Nick Lidgett.

"You're back," Lidgett said. "Beer?"

"Definitely."

Lidgett drew Clint a cold one and set it in front of him.

"Anything happen while I was gone?" Clint asked.

"If you're talking about the Starrs, the status is the same. Belle is still alive; Sam is still at her side."

"That's good. Nothing else going on in town?"

"Not a thing," Lidgett said. "It's been quiet. But then, it's a quiet town."

"Belle Starr getting shot?" Clint asked. "That's your idea of being quiet?"

"That happened outside of town," the bartender said, "not in, remember?"

"Oh, yeah."

Lidgett leaned on the bar.

"What'd you find out?"

"When?" Clint asked.

"Wherever you've been the last couple of days." Lidgett said. "Fort Smith, maybe?"

"What makes you say that?"

Lidgett stood up straight and spread his arms.

"Where else is there to go that's different from here?" he asked. "You talk to Judge Parker?"

"Only when I have to," Clint said. "Now why would you ask about Parker?"

"Parker hates Belle and Sam Starr," Lidgett said, "and Bass Reeves was in town. You know Reeves, so I'm willing to bet you know Parker. Am I warm?"

"You ever been a lawman? Or a detective?"

"Neither one."

"You're missing your calling."

"So you talked to Parker about Belle?"

"He doesn't care that she got shot," Clint said, "doesn't want Bass working on it."

"But?"

"But he is," Clint said. "He hasn't been back while I was gone, has he?"

"No," Lidgett said.

"Okay, here's another one for you. Do you know a man named Butler?"

"No. Why, who is he?"

"Just a name I came across."

"Ah, is he the one who's supposed to have shot Belle?" Lidgett said. "I can ask around."

"Good idea," Clint said. "I'll check back with you tomorrow night."

He finished his beer.

"'nother one?" Lidgett asked.

"No, thanks," Clint said. "I'm going to my hotel room and read a book."

Chapter Thirty-Three

He may have meant to go to his room to read a book, but when he woke up the next morning, he realized he'd simply fallen asleep. When he saw his gunbelt on the bedpost, he was relieved that at least he'd remembered to do that before nodding off.

He woke the next morning feeling old. What other reason would there be for him to drift off like that? A hard day's ride never used to do that to him.

After washing up and getting dressed, he went out for breakfast, hoping that a good one would give him some energy to get through the day.

After steak-and-eggs, he hit the streets for his search for the man named Butler. But first he went over to Doc Hewitt's to check on Belle Starr.

***

Sam Starr came to his feet fast when Clint entered the office, his hand going for his gun.

"Take it easy, Starr," Clint said.

"Oh, it's you." Starr settled back into his chair. "When did you get back?"

"Last night. How is she doing?"

"Doc says she's gonna make it," Starr said. "But it'll be a while before she's up and around."

"Well, that's good," Clint said. "Why don't you go on home and get some rest?"

"Not home," Starr said, "but I may sleep in a hotel and then come back." He stood up. "What did you find out?"

"Do you know a man named Butler?"

"Brad Butler?"

"I don't know," Clint sad. "All I got was Butler."

"Brad Butler rode with us for a while, until Belle kicked him out," Starr said. "He was mad as hell, said he'd get back at her. Did he shoot her?"

"I know someone named Butler is involved," Clint said. "He got a telegram from Detroit telling him to go ahead. I don't know if he did the shooting, or had somebody do it."

"Knowing Butler, he had somebody else do it."

"Do you know where I can find him?"

"No idea," Starr said, "but when you do, let me have him."

"Give me a guess, Sam," Clint said. "Would he be here, or in Fort Smith?"

"If he's involved with the shootin', he'll stay around here to make sure it gets done."

"Okay, good," Clint said. "I'll keep looking."

"You gonna talk to the Doc?" Starr asked.

"Yeah, before I leave."

"Tell 'im I'll be back after I get a coupla hours sleep, will ya?"

"I will."

"And Adams," Starr said, "thanks for what you're doin'."

"Thank me when I catch the shooter," Clint said.

Starr left, and Clint waited for Doc Hewitt to come out of the other room.

"Oh, Adams." The doctor looked around. "Good, you got Starr to leave."

"He's getting a couple of hours sleep," Clint said, "but he'll be back."

"Well, maybe after some sleep he'll stop glarin' at me like I'm the one who shot Belle."

"I came up with a name for him," Clint said, "so I don't think you have to worry."

"What name?"

"Butler," he said. "Starr said it might be someone named Brad Butler."

"Don't know him," Hewitt said.

"How is she, Doc?"

"She's made it this far, so it looks good," Hewitt said.

"Then you saved her."

"I think she saved herself," the doctor said. "She's just too tough to give in."

"Good for her." Clint was glad he wasn't going to have to tell Roxy Doyle that her friend got killed on his watch.

"She'd probably improve even more if you could tell her you got the person who shot her."

"I'm working on it, Doc," Clint said. "I'm working on it."

***

Brad Butler waited in the Blind Duck, probably the town's most rundown saloon. It specialized in dirty glasses, but it was a good place to meet if you didn't want to be seen.

Butler was waiting for two men—Mike Barry and Ted White. Both men were guns for hire and, apparently, they hadn't gotten the job done.

Butler had gotten the word from Detroit to make sure Belle Starr was dead. He would like to have shot her himself, but he couldn't take the chance. She might recognize him and see him coming. But she and Sam Starr didn't know Mike Barry or Ted White, so it made sense to farm the job out to them.

When the two men walked in, they spotted Butler right away. Barry walked over to him, while White went to the bar for two beers.

"She's alive," Butler said to Mike Barry.

"That's what we heard," Barry said, sitting. "Don't get upset, we'll see that she don't walk outta the doctor's office."

Ted White came over with the beer, handed one to his partner, and remained standing. The two men were in their thirties, but were very different. Ted White had too much energy to ever sit still, while Mike Barry had a laid back, laconic attitude that rarely changed.

"Oh yeah? When?"

"Soon," Barry said. "Sam Starr's been sittin' in there with her the whole time."

"Well," Butler said, "kill him, too."

"And the doc?" White asked.

"No, don't kill the doc," Butler said.

"Okay, then," Barry said, "just leave it to us, Butler. We'll get it done."

"Well, when you do, meet me here and you'll get the rest of your money."

"Oh, we'll be here," Ted White said. "You just make sure you got our money."

"Why didn't you make sure she was dead the first time?" Butler demanded. "Then we wouldn't still be here, worryin' about the Gunsmith."

"We each put a bullet into her," Barry said. "That shoulda been enough. As for Adams, don't worry about him. We can handle him."

"What makes you so sure?" Butler said.

"His day is done," Barry said. "He's a legend, ain't he? That means he's gettin' old."

"Bein' called a legend is the worst thing that can happen to ya," Ted White said. "Means yer windin' down, yer time is done."

"Well, for all our sakes I hope you're right," Brad Butler said.

"Yeah," Barry said, "I think I'd worry more about Sam Starr, or even Belle herself, than the Gunsmith."

Ted White drained his dirty beer mug and slammed it down on the table.

"We gotta go, Mike," White said.

Barry nodded, finished his beer and slowly stood up, setting his mug down next to his partner's.

"Remember, Butler," he said, "just be here with the rest of our money."

"I'll have it," Butler answered. "And get the job done, this time."

The two gunnies left the saloon and Butler wondered if he should risk his health by having a drink there?

Chapter Thirty-Four

Clint left Doc Hewitt's feeling a certain amount of satisfaction. Belle was going to pull through, and he now knew who he was looking for.

But there was something else, something that he wished he'd thought of while in Fort Smith. If Starr was right and Butler was farming the job out, that meant he had to pay the shooters. If the job was coming from Detroit, then Butler would probably have to pick some money up at a bank in order to pay the shooters.

Clint didn't know how much of a bank Eufaula had. But a Fort Smith bank would certainly have had enough cash on hand. He should've checked the bank there before leaving, or had Deputy Magnus do it. If Helen Magnus managed to send him a messenger, he'd get that message back to her.

As he left the doctor's office, he thought about going back in to ask Hewitt about the bank, but instead he decided to just go there and check, himself.

As he walked, he wondered when Bass Reeves would be coming back. If he hadn't caught up to the shooters by now, then where was he? Hopefully he wasn't chasing their trail halfway across the territories. Clint had the feeling that, with the job not done right the first time, they'd still be around.

When he found the bank, he felt sure he was right about it not having enough cash on hand to pay for the job. It wasn't much more than a shack with the word BANK above the door. Just to make sure he went inside, found a single teller behind one window, quickly discovered that the small man was also the bank manager.

"No, sir," he said, to Clint's question, "we ain't had a request for cash in some time. All we ever get is some storekeepers depositing their day's receipts, which ain't never much." He looked around and added quite sheepishly, "You can see, we ain't much of a bank."

Clint had that thought himself, already.

"Well then, you've got one good thing going for you," Clint said.

"What's that, sir?"

"There's not much chance of you being robbed, is there?" Clint asked.

The bank manager laughed.

"You're probably right about that," he said. Then, as Clint was leaving, he called out, "Can I interest you in opening an account?"

Chapter Thirty-Five

Clint left the bank, looked up and down the street, and saw a rider coming in. At first he thought it might be Magnus' messenger, but then he recognized Bass Reeves. He stepped out into the street and Reeves reined in.

"You look like you need a drink," he said.

"A beer and a steak."

"I'll buy," Clint said.

***

They went to the nearest café, easily got a table they wanted because it was between meals, and sat. Reeves looked exhausted, but when his beer came, he guzzled half of it, and when his steak came, he attacked it with vigor.

Clint had a beer in front of him, and watched Reeves eat.

"I finally realized," Reeves said, "that the trail circled around and led back here."

"It took you this long to realize that?" Clint asked. "That's not like you, Bass."

"I know," Reeves said. "These men were pros. How's Belle?"

"Alive."

"If they're pros, why is she alive?" Reeves asked.

"They each put a slug into her," Clint said. "They must've just thought that would be enough."

"And then they led me a merry chase," Reeves said, "makin' me feel like a fool."

"So they came back here," Clint said, "because the job's not done. They're going to try for her again."

Reeves pushed his plate away.

"What are you going to do?" Clint asked.

"Take a bath, and a long nap," Reeves said, "and then decide. What've you been doin'?"

"I went to Fort Smith, met Deputy Magnus—"

"The Judge's lady deputy," Reeves said.

"Yes," Clint said, "she's helping."

"And how did the judge take that?"

"Probably not well," Clint said. "He doesn't care that Belle got shot, but Magnus swears she won't let him stop her."

"Magnus?"

"Deputy, whatever you want to call her."

"I think," Reeves said, "after I get some sleep, I'm going to have more questions."

"You can go to my hotel for your bath, and then use my room," Clint said. "I'm still searching the town for a man named Butler."

"Brad Butler?"

"You know him?"

"He's for hire," Reeves said. "He's worked with Indians, Comancheros, you name it."

"Do you know what he looks like?"

"I do," Reeves said. "He's tall and homely lookin', saddest lookin' man I've ever seen."

"Seems like I'll know him when I see him," Clint said.

"I can help you look—"

"Sure you can," Clint said, "but after you've had some rest."

"You're right," Reeves said. "I won't be any good to you in this condition."

They left the cafe and walked to Clint's hotel, where he gave Bass Reeves the key to his room.

"I'll see you when you wake up," Clint said.

"If somethin' happens and you need back-up, wake me," Reeves said.

"Oh, I will," Clint promised.

He went back to the street.

***

Now that he had a description of Brad Butler, he covered old ground, checking streets, stores, saloons, and cafes. He finished up in the Last Race Saloon where Nick Lidgett gave him a cold beer.

"You look like you can use it," Lidgett said, "on the house."

"Thanks."

"Still lookin' for whoever shot Belle Starr?"

"Yes," Clint said, "and I have an idea who's behind it."

"This Butler you asked me about?"

"Yeah," Clint said, "only I've got a description now." He told Lidgett what bass Reeves had told him.

"I've seen that guy!" the bartender said.

"Where?"

"In here."

"When?"

"Oh," Lidgett said, "A while back. I thought he was the saddest man I'd ever seen."

"That's him," Clint said. "What was he doing here?"

"Having a beer, same as you," Lidgett said. "Standin' right here at the bar."

"Did he talk to anyone?"

"Not a soul, that I remember."

"So he was here to drink, not do business."

"I'd say so," the bartender agreed.

"So where would he go to do business?" Clint asked. "To meet with somebody where he didn't want to be seen?"

Lidgett thought a few moments, then snapped his fingers and said, "I got just the place."

Chapter Thirty-Six

Clint approached the Blind Duck Saloon, and saw what Nick Lidgett had meant when he said nobody would actually go there to drink.

"Do yourself a favor," Lidgett said, "and don't have a drink there. Folks in town say they specialize in dirty glasses."

"Then why are they still open?"

"For just the reason you're lookin' for," Lidgett said. "Someplace for people to meet where decent folks won't see 'em."

As Clint approached the batwing doors, he saw that he had to go through them carefully, as one was hanging by a single rusty hinge. He entered and looked around. Two tables were taken, with two men each seated at them. None of them was a homely, sad looking man.

He went up to the bar, where a bored looking bartender waited.

"What can I getcha?" he asked.

Clint looked at the bar top, ran his fingers over it, then wiped them on his trousers.

"You're kidding, right?"

"Then whataya want?"

"I'm looking for somebody."

"Order a beer," the bartender said.

"I won't drink it."

"I don't care if you pour it on the floor," the bartender said. "Order it."

"I'll have a beer."

"Comin' up."

The bartender drew a beer and set it down in front of Clint, who could see what people meant about the dirty glasses. Some of the grime was actually floating on top.

"Who ya lookin' for?" the bartender asked.

"A fella named Butler, Brad Butler."

"Don't know 'im."

"He's the saddest looking man you've ever seen."

"Oh, him!"

"He's been here?"

The bartender stared at him, then said, "Order a shot of whiskey."

"I'll have a shot."

The bartender poured him a grimy shot, which he ignored.

"When was he here?" Clint asked.

"Earlier today."

"Anybody with him?"

"Two men."

"Did you know them?"

"No."

"Can you describe them?"

The bartender looked at the two drinks in front of Clint.

"I'll have another beer," Clint said.

"I thought you might."

He placed another beer in front of Clint, went on to describe the two men.

"Have they been in before?"

"Once, last week," the man said.

That must have been when they got the job of shooting Belle Starr. Today must have been them getting the word to finish it.

Clint put some money on the bar and said, "Thanks."

"Thank *you*," the bartender said, picking up the money. "Come again."

Clint left and went directly to Doc Hewitt's.

***

If Bass Reeves wasn't so tuckered out, he might have woke him and asked him to sit with Belle Starr. Instead, he entered the doctor's office, took a seat, and figured to sit there until Sam Starr showed up, again.

Doc Hewitt came out of his examination room.

"What's going on?" he asked.

"I'm expecting another attempt on Belle," Clint said. "So I'll be here for a while."

"Until Sam shows up?"

"Right."

"Should I have a gun ready?" Hewitt asked.

"If you know how to use it."

"I find the determination to use a gun is often more important than the skill," Doc Hewitt said.

"That's a good point, Doc."

"I'll tuck it into my belt," Hewitt said, "just in case."

"You'll only need it if they get past me," Clint advised him.

"And what are the chances of that?" Hewitt asked.

"None."

"That's what I thought."

"How is she?" Clint asked.

"I'm expecting her to wake up any minute," Hewitt said. "I'll ask her."

Chapter Thirty-Seven

About twenty minutes later Hewitt stuck his head out the door.

"She's awake."

"Can I talk to her?" Clint asked.

"Come ahead."

Clint got up and entered the room, saw Belle lying on her back on a table. There was a lamp next to it, and a round disc of shiny metal above her, to reflect and intensify the light.

Both men stared down at her.

"How are you feeling?" Clint asked.

"Like I been kicked by a mule," she said, "twice. What happened?"

"I was hoping you could tell me," Clint said. "You got shot, twice."

"Oh." She swallowed. "I remember the first bullet hittin' me. Not the second."

"Do you remember falling off your horse?" Clint asked.

"No."

"So you didn't see anybody, then?"

"No one," she said. "I was just . . . ridin'."

"Do you know a jasper named Bart Butler?"

"No," she said. "Did he shoot me?"

"He hired it done," Clint said.

"Why?"

"I don't know," Clint said, "but the word came from Detroit."

She licked her lips before answering.

"That figures."

"Here," Hewitt said, and held her head so she could drink some water.

"W-where's Sam?" she asked.

"He's been here ever since you got shot," Hewitt said. "I finally got him to go and get some sleep by telling him you'll be okay."

"He'll be back any minute," Clint assured her. "He's been worried sick."

"Really?"

"Did you think he wouldn't be?"

"H–has he been . . ."

"Drinking?" Clint asked. "Not a drop since you got shot."

"Well, that's good." She closed her eyes.

"Okay," Hewitt said, "that's enough. Let her rest."

Clint nodded. As he withdrew from the room, he realized she had fallen asleep.

***

When Sam Starr walked in, he looked tired, but a hundred per cent better than he'd looked before.

"How is she?" he asked.

"She woke up briefly," Clint said, "asked for you."

"What'd you tell her?"

"The truth," Clint said. "That you've been sitting here since she got shot, haven't had a drop to drink, and the doctor finally convinced you to get some rest."

"What'd she say?"

"That made her happy," Clint said, "then she went to sleep."

"Did she see anythin'?" he asked.

"She only remembers being hit by the first bullet," Clint said. "Nothing before or after."

"Damn. What are you doin' here?"

Clint told Starr what he'd found out in the last few hours, and why he felt the need to sit in the office and wait for Starr to come back.

"If they come here," Starr swore, "I'll be ready."

"Good," Clint said, "but maybe I can find them and head them off."

"I hope for their sake," Starr said, "you can."

Clint hit the streets again, this time looking for three men. He would have settled for finding one of the three. But a complete circuit of the town revealed nothing. If the men were there, they were in hiding. Or possibly camping out of town.

***

It had been several hours since Bass Reeves had ridden back in. Clint wondered if it was a good time to wake the man? Or simply walking down the hall outside the room would tell. If it was him, he'd hear the floor creaking and know somebody was coming. He had to expect at least the same awareness from a man like Deputy Marshal Bass Reeves.

Clint entered the hotel, went up the stairs and walked down the hall, making no attempt at silence. He stopped in front of Reeves' door and listened.

"Yeah, yeah." He heard Bass Reeves say, "I hear you pounding around out there, Adams. Come on in."

Clint opened the door and entered.

"How'd you know it was me?"

"Who else would have the nerve to wake me?" Reeves asked. He was sitting on the bed, pulling on his boots. "Fill me in on what's been happenin' while I was asleep."

Clint did, including his theory about the shooters camping outside of town.

"Let me guess," Reeves said. "You want me to get on my horse again and check the area."

"Well," Clint said, "I did give you my bed."

"You know," the deputy said, standing up, "Judge Parker's gonna have my ass. I should've checked in days ago."

"Well then, one additional day, more or less, isn't going to make him any happier."

"'Happy' is not a word we associate with Judge Isaac Parker," Reeves said. "The only time anybody ever seen him smiling is when he's lookin' out his window, watchin' a hangin'."

Chapter Thirty-Eight

Clint and Bass Reeves left the hotel at the same time. Reeves stopped at the desk to tell the clerk to have the sheets changed in Mr. Adams' room.

"I sweat when I sleep," he told Clint.

"Thanks for the thought."

Out on the street they stopped, and Reeves said, "I'll see if I can get a fresh horse from the livery."

"I'll pay for it."

"No need," Reeves said, "I'll use my badge to appropriate one. I'll return it when I'm done."

"Sounds good to me," Clint said. "I'll come along."

At the livery they made arrangements for Reeves fresh mount, and then walked the horse outside. Reeves mounted up.

"If you find them," Clint said, "come back and get me and I'll—"

"No offense, Clint," Reeves said, "but if I find 'em I'll just do my job."

"Fine. Will you stop here again before going back to Fort Smith?"

"Yes," Reeves said. "I'll let you know what happens, and you do the same."

"Agreed."

Clint reached up and shook hands with Reeves.

"Thanks, Deputy."

Reeves nodded, turned his horse and rode out of town.

***

It was several hours later when another rider came into town. Clint was still on the street, studying faces, and stopped to watch.

The rider saw him, seemed to recognize him, and rode over.

"Mr. Adams?"

"That's right."

"I've been sent by Deputy Magnus."

"Her messenger?"

"Yes, sir," he said.

"Can I have the message?"

"She wrote it down," the man said. "I was to give it only to you."

"Okay then," Clint said, "I'll take it."

The man took a piece of paper from his pocket and started to hand it over.

"How did you know I was, uh, me?" Clint asked.

"She described you to me, sir," the man said.

"Okay," Clint said, accepting the message.

It said, in a neat and precise handwriting: NO BUTLER HERE. OVER TO YOU.

"Any return message?" the man asked.

"Yes," Clint said, "tell her thanks. I'll take it from here."

"Yes, sir."

The man turned his horse.

"Don't you want to rest first?" Clint asked.

"No, sir," the man said. "I have to get back before Judge Parker misses me."

"Then thanks," Clint said.

The man waved and spurred his horse on.

Now it was up to him to find Butler and his shooters.

***

Clint had only spoken to the self-appointed constable, Frank West, that one time in the street in front of his hotel. If anyone in town wanted the Starrs shot and killed, it would be him.

Clint found West eating in the best restaurant in town—which wasn't saying much.

"Adams," West said. "I'm finishing a very good steak. Would you like one?"

"Maybe later," Clint said. "Somewhere else with somebody else."

"Suit yourself." He continued to cut up his meat. "What can I do for you?"

"Brad Butler."

"What about him?"

"I understand you know him," Clint lied.

"I don't know where you heard that."

"Do you know where he is?" Clint asked.

West looked up from his plate.

"What makes you think I'd know that?"

"Maybe because nobody else knows it."

"You're not makin' any sense," West said, going back to his meal.

"It's general knowledge that you and Sam Starr don't get along," Clint said. "In my book, that makes you a suspect in Belle's shooting."

"You're crazy," West said. "I have nothin' against Belle."

"Are you sure?"

"I'm positive," West said. "So if Sam Starr gets shot, come and see me. Otherwise, I'd like to finish my supper."

A waiter came over and looked at Clint.

"Bring me what he's having."

Chapter Thirty-Nine

"Why set yourself up as an unofficial constable?" Clint asked.

"There's no law here."

"Judge Parker's deputies—"

"Like I said," West interrupted, "no law."

"Okay," Clint said, "let's say you're on the level. You really want to be the law here. Why the feud with Sam Starr?"

West gestured with his steak knife.

"Because I'm on one side of the law, and he's on the other."

"But he served his time."

"And it's only a matter of time before he crosses over, again," West said. "And I'm gonna be here."

"To catch him?" Clint asked. "Or kill him?"

West shrugged.

"Catch him, kill him, that's up to him."

"And what about Belle?"

"One Starr at a time," West said.

Clint cut into his steak, found it delicious. By the time they finished their supper, he had more accrued respect for Frank West than he would have thought after their first meeting.

***

They left the restaurant together, stopped outside.

"The saddest lookin' man I ever saw?" he asked. "You're sure?"

"That's what I'm told."

"And his name is Brad Butler."

"Right."

"I'll be on the lookout for him," West said. "So, are we workin' together on this now?"

"Yes," Clint said, "you, me, Bass Reeves and a deputy named Magnus."

"Magnus," West said. "Never heard of him, but I know Reeves."

"Bass is out there beating the bushes," Clint said, "so that leaves town for you and me."

"I appreciate you clueing me in, Adams."

"Well, it started out because I didn't trust you," Clint said.

"And now you do?"

"Let's just say my opinion's changed, a bit."

***

Brad Butler walked into the Blind Duck Saloon after dark and frowned as the bartender began waving at him.

"What the hell—" he said, as he reached the bar.

"You gotta get outta here!" the bartender told him. "Right away."

"Why?"

"Clint Adams was in here lookin' for ya today."

"Are you sure it was Adams?" Butler asked.

"Well, first Adams and then Frank West," the barman said. "You ain't afraid of West, are ya?"

"I hardly know him," Butler said.

"But you know who the Gunsmith is, right?"

"Well, of course."

"Well, he's lookin' for ya and I don't want him to find ya here."

"Why not?" Butler asked. "The gunplay might break some of your dirty glasses?"

"I don't want Clint Adams comin' here no more," the bartender said.

"What'd you tell him about me?" Butler asked.

"Nothin'," the bartender lied. "I didn't tell 'im nothin', and I ain't gonna."

Butler wished he could believe the bartender, but the man was such a talker, it was fortunate the saloon didn't do very much business.

"Have you seen Mike Barry or Ted White since the last time they were in here with me?"

"Nope."

Butler was worried. The word he'd gotten was that Deputy Marshal Bass Reeves was out looking for camps in the area. If he found Barry and White, there'd be a problem. The two men felt certain they could handle Clint Adams, but Adams and Reeves might be a problem.

He had to find them first.

***

Clint and West went their separate ways, agreeing to call on the man if he needed to. Sam Starr might not like it, but West was willing to help save Belle Starr's life, if the shooters tried again.

Clint decided to go back to Doc Hewitt's, check on Belle Starr's condition, and check in with Sam Starr to see if he needed anything.

Chapter Forty

"I was just in there talkin' to her," Starr said. "She sounded okay."

"Well, one of us better stay in here at all times," Clint said. "If the word gets out that she's talking, they're definitely going to try again."

"I'll stay here," Starr said. "It's my job to protect my wife."

"Okay," Clint said, "then I'll just keep looking for the shooters on the street."

"That's not your job," Starr said. "Why don't you just . . . pull out."

"I still owe Roxy Doyle my help," Clint said. "That means I owe it to Belle, and, by extension, that means I owe it to you, too."

"Well," Starr said, "I ain't gonna argue with ya. I'm just gonna say thanks for whatever you can do."

"Thank me when it's over," Clint said. "By the way, Frank West is willing to help."

"What? West? Yeah, he wants to help me into an early grave."

"That may be the case," Clint said, "but he doesn't want Belle dead."

"Or so he told you."

"Yeah, he did."

"Well, it's up to you if you wanna believe 'im," Starr said. "But if I was you, I'd watch my back around him."

"Okay," Clint said, "I'll keep that in mind."

He left the doctor's office.

***

Bass Reeves rode around the town in ever widening circles, hoping to see or smell somebody's camp. When he finally found it, there was nobody there, and the ashes of the dead fire were still warm. It was possible someone warned them he was coming, somebody from town, but who? Who knew he was out there searching but Clint Adams?

The hostler at the livery stable.

***

Butler had gotten to White and Barry just in time. They broke camp, kicked the fire to death, and got out of there.

"Why don't we just kill Reeves?" Barry asked.

"Because he's a lawman," Butler said. "You don't kill lawmen."

"Why not?" Ted White asked. "Seems to me that's exactly who we should be killin'."

"Because if you kill a lawman," Butler said, "it brings other lawmen down on you. We don't need that."

"What if he gets too close?" Mike Barry asked.

"That's different," Butler said. "Then we'd have no choice. Right now we have a choice."

"And that is?" White asked.

"Avoid Bass Reeves."

***

Reeves rode back to town, found Clint. He told him what he'd found.

"Just the one campsite?" Clint asked.

"That's it."

"And you think the guy at the livery told them about you?" Clint went on.

"Unless you did."

"I haven't told anybody what we're doing," Clint said, then paused.

"What is it?" Reeves asked.

"I did tell Sam Starr."

"He's her husband," Reeves said. "Why would he have told anybody anythin'?"

"He wouldn't," Clint said.

"So let's visit the livery."

***

"I just told him that the deputy rode out," the hostler said. "Ya know, just making conversation."

"And who was this you told?" Clint asked.

"Just a fella I drink with sometimes," the man said. "His name's Lester Dent."

"Where can we find this Dent?" Reeves asked.

"This time of day?" the hostler said. "In a saloon."

***

The hostler gave them a description, and they found their man standing at the bar in a small saloon called the Cactus. They approached and took up a position on either side of him. Dent was tall and nervous looking, and seemed even more nervous as he looked from Clint to Reeves, and back.

"Hello, Deputy," he said, speaking to Reeves because he saw the badge on his chest.

"Are you Lester Dent?" Reeves asked.

"That's me," Dent said. "What can I do for you fellers?"

"You heard that I was ridin' out to look for camps in the area," Reeves said. "We need to know who you told."

"Huh? I didn't tell nobody."

"Come on," Clint said. "What I hear is you'll talk to anybody who stands you a drink."

Dent looked at Clint, then looked at the warm remnants of the beer in his mug.

Clint waved at the bartender and said, "Give my friend a fresh beer."

Dent smiled as the bartender set a new beer in front of him. When he started to reach for it, though, Reeves slapped his big hand down on the man's wrist.

"Hold on," Clint said. "First, we need an answer to our question. You must have told somebody about Reeves riding out."

"Well," Dent said, sheepishly, "I might've mentioned it to a fella named Butler."

Clint and Reeves exchanged a glance behind the man's head.

"If you can tell me where to find Butler," Clint said to Dent, "I'll add a shot of whiskey to this beer."

Dent's face actually fell, and that was when Clint knew they had gotten what they could out of him. Reeves knew, too, and released Dent's hand.

"That's okay," Clint said to Dent, then looked at the bartender. "Give him a shot, anyway."

Clint dropped some money on the bar, then he and Reeves headed for the batwing doors.

Chapter Forty-One

Outside the saloon Clint said, "At least we know Butler's in town."

"Or was," Reeves said.

"I think as long as Belle's alive, he'll be around."

"And his two shooters?" Reeves asked.

"They've got to be," Clint said. "It doesn't seem likely Butler would finish the job himself, when he farmed it out to begin with."

Reeves looked out at the street.

"This ain't a big town," he said. "I doubt they would've just switched their camp. If Butler warned them, then they're in town, somewhere."

"And who is he," Clint said.

"So how do we get them to come out of hidin'?" Reeves asked.

"That's easy," Clint said.

"Is it?"

"We just put Belle Starr on the street."

"Can she walk?"

"I doubt it."

"Then how—oh, I get it."

Clint nodded.

"You think you can find a girl who looks like Belle in this town?" Reeves asked.

"We'd find one in Fort Smith. But it'd take a while to do that and then get her here," Clint said.

"So it's out of the question, then," Reeves said. "What's next?"

"Giving them a chance to get to her in the doc's office," Clint said.

"Do you think you can convince them she's in there alone?" Reeves asked.

"Or just with the doc," Clint said, "only I don't want to put him at risk."

"Then how will you play it?"

"I'm not sure," Clint said. "I'll have to give it some thought."

"Well, you do that," Reeves said, "and I'll get my own hotel room, just in case it takes a day or two."

"Isn't the Judge expecting you back?"

Reeves smiled.

"Days ago," he said. "Let him wait."

"I appreciate that, Bass," Clint said.

"Besides," Reeves added, "he's got his lady deputy to play with."

"You got something against her?" Clint asked.

"She's a rich woman playin' at bein' a deputy," Reeves said. "It's a job I take serious."

"Can she do the job?" Clint asked.

"I ain't worked with her."

"Because you don't want to?"

"Because Parker knows better," Reeves said, and left it at that.

"All right," Clint said, "well, get your room, and I'll go and see Belle at the doc's."

"Sam Starr there, too?"

"He better be," Clint said "He told me he'd be watching her the whole time."

"I'll see you at the hotel, then," Reeves said.

"Fine," Clint said. "We'll get some supper later, and I'll let you know if I've come up with a plan."

Reeves nodded, stepped off the boardwalk and headed for the hotel.

Clint gave Reeves a head start, watched the street to see if anyone was watching him or the deputy. Satisfied that there was nobody on either of the trails, he stepped into the street and started for the doctor's office.

Chapter Forty-Two

"You wanna what?" Sam Starr asked. "Use Belle as bait?"

"Without putting her in any danger."

"How do you think you can do that?" Starr asked.

"By making people *think* she's here all alone," Clint explained.

"How're you gonna do that?"

"Well, we'll let them see you leave by the front door," Clint said, "then the doctor can leave the same way."

"And?"

"And I come in the back and wait."

"And where do I go when I leave?" Starr asked.

"You can go home."

"Try again."

"You could go around the back and come back in," Clint said.

"I like that better. And where's your friend, Bass Reeves, gonna be?"

"Oh, somewhere within earshot," Clint said.

"So he can hear the shots?"

"Right."

"And when do you wanna do this?"

"I think they're probably just waiting for a chance," Clint said, "so we can probably set it up for tomorrow."

"And how are you gonna get the word out?"

"I'll do some drinking at the saloons tonight," Clint said, "and run my mouth."

"Well, that ain't gonna work," Starr said.

"Why's that?" Clint asked.

"Because you ain't the type," Starr said. "Nobody's gonna believe that you're gettin' drunk and talkin' too much."

"You might be right," Clint said. "Maybe I can get Reeves to do it."

"Are you kiddin'? There's even less chance people'll believe he's gettin' drunk."

"Then what do you suggest?"

"I been drunk in these saloons more times than I can count," Starr said. "So I'll go in tonight and do some talkin'."

"Well," Clint said, "that's a good idea, Sam. And I'll stay here and watch over Belle until you get back."

"But you're gonna supply the money for the drinks, right?" Starr asked.

"Oh, definitely," Clint said. "The drinks are all on me."

***

Clint and Starr made arrangements for Clint to come back after dark. Then Clint went back to his hotel to collect Reeves for supper. He figured he'd inform Reeves of the plans over their meal. The desk clerk told him Reeves' room number, and he went up. Reeves was in room eleven, just down the hall on the same side as Clint's.

The big deputy opened the door and let him in.

"That was quick," Reeves said.

"Well, I didn't talk to Belle, she was still out, but I talked with Sam."

"Come up with a plan?"

"I did," Clint said. "Come on, I'll tell you over a meal. I've got just the place picked out."

Clint and Reeves left the hotel and Clint led the way to the Cajun Café.

"Cajun food?" Reeves asked. "Here?"

"It surprised me, too," Clint admitted, "but it's pretty good."

They got as isolated a table as possible, but there were still people around them, eyeing them curiously.

"It's either my badge, or my skin," Bass Reeves said, "or your reputation that's attractin' attention."

"It doesn't matter which," Clint said. "Nobody here is going to do anything but look."

The waiter came over to the table and remembered Clint from the first time he was there.

"Welcome back," he said. "And you brought a friend."

"I told him about the food and he wanted to try it himself," Clint said.

"What did you have in mind?" the waiter asked Reeves.

"Jambalaya?"

"Ah, excellent choice. And you, sir?"

"It was good the first time, so I'll have the same again," Clint said.

"Two jambalayas coming up," the waiter said.

"And two beers," Clint said.

"Yes, sir."

They drank some of their beer and Clint told Reeves his plan while they waited for their food.

"It sounds too simple," Reeves said. "Do you think it'll work?"

"I think it's too simple, too," Clint said, "so I've added something."

"What?"

"You and I are going to make it look like we're leaving town."

Chapter Forty-Three

After supper Clint went back to Doc Hewitt's office, found the doctor in conversation with Sam Starr.

"Adams," Hewitt said, "Sam's told me what you're planning. I'm not sure I want to go along with it."

"All you have to do, Doctor, is go home and stay safe," Clint said.

"I have to be here tomorrow for my other patients," Hewitt said, "and for anyone who might fall ill or be injured."

"That's fine, then," Clint said. "It'll be you and me, unless we can move Belle?"

"No, not yet," Hewitt said. "Maybe in a couple of days."

"And by then she could be dead," Starr said, "shot again. I wanna go along with Adams' plan, Doc. I'll come in the back and we'll all be here."

"Yes, all right," Hewitt said. "What do we do now?"

"You go home," Clint said, "and Sam goes drinking, then comes back. Hopefully, tomorrow, the shooters will try again, and we'll have them."

"Yes, all right," Hewitt said, "but I want it agreed that if anything else happens to Belle Starr, I'm in no way to blame."

"Agreed," Sam Starr said. "Guess it's time for me to go and be drunk."

Starr left and Hewitt stared at Clint.

"What?"

"You just sent that man to a saloon to get drunk."

"Pretend to get drunk."

"Sam Starr's never pretended to be drunk in his life," Hewitt said.

"Well, tell you what, Doc," Clint said. "Whether he pretends or not, as long as he talks, this plan goes into effect."

Doc Hewitt put his jacket on.

"I'm going home," he said. "I just hope my patient lives through tomorrow."

As the doc went out the door, Clint was hoping that his patient would live through the night.

***

As it got later and later and Sam Starr hadn't returned, Clint started to worry about what the doctor said. If Starr started drinking for real, the plan might go awry.

Clint made sure the back door was unlocked, and when he heard it open, he hoped it would be a Sam Starr who wasn't too drunk.

"Adams?" he heard.

"Here, Sam."

Starr appeared from the back. As he came into the light Clint saw that the man looked sober. As he got closer, he also smelled sober.

"How did it go?" Clint asked.

"Good, I think. I started drinkin', then talked about headin' home tomorrow because it looked like Belle was gonna make it."

"And me and Reeves?"

"I talked about how you was both leavin' in the mornin'," Starr said.

"Anybody say anything?"

"A few fellas congratulated me on Belle makin' it," Starr said. "A coupla others said they was glad you and Reeves was leavin' town. Maybe there'd be no more trouble."

"Really?" Clint said. "What the hell did Reeves and I have to do with any of the trouble? Never mind. It doesn't matter. Do you know a fellow named Dent?"

"Lester? Sure."

"Was he in the saloon?"

"Yah, he was tryin' to get some free drinks."

"Good," Clint said. "I get the feeling he'll carry the word for us."

"You're probably right," Starr said. "Lester'll do any-thin' for a drink."

"I'm heading back to my hotel, now. I'll check out early in the morning and ride out with Reeves. Don't forget to leave that back door unlocked."

"You don't think they'll try for Belle tonight, in the dark?" Starr asked.

"I think it'll take time for the word to get to them, and then for them to form a plan. No, I think tomorrow's going to be soon enough."

"Okay, then," Starr said. "I'll see ya in the mornin'."

Clint nodded, and went out the front door. He paused just outside to look up and down the dark street, and to let his eyes adjust to the darkness outside. Then he headed for his hotel.

***

As Clint had presumed, it was Lester Dent who carried the word to Brad Butler. Butler had found a deserted cabin to take shelter in, along with Ted White and Mike Barry. When Lester appeared at the door, White and Barry were sleeping in a corner on their bedrolls.

"What do you have for me, Lester?" Butler asked.

"Sam Starr was in the Last Race, drinkin' and talkin' about how Belle pulled through, thanks to Doc Hewitt."

"Is she going home?" Butler asked.

"No, but Sam is. He's gonna head home tomorrow, get some fresh clothes and some sleep, and then come back later in the day."

"So she'll be there with the doc," Butler said. "What about Adams, and that deputy, Reeves?"

"That's the real good news for ya, Butler," Dent said. "They're leavin' town early."

"Both of them?"

"Yup," Dent said. "Ain't that worth a coupla drinks?"

"It's worth a beer," Butler said, handing Dent two bits, "but if Adams and Reeves really do ride out early, it'll be worth more."

"So what I gotta do, watch 'em?" Dent asked.

"That's right," Butler said, "and if you see them ride out, you come and let me know. There's a bottle in it for you."

Dent cackled happily.

"That'll be a cinch, Butler. A cinch, I tellya."

"Just make sure you didn't make a mistake," Butler said.

"I will, I swear I'll make sure," Dent said. "I'll see ya in the mornin' for that bottle."

Dent left and Butler locked the door. He looked over at White and Barry, decided to let them sleep. If he got the news in the morning that he wanted, he'd tell them. Right now, he'd just get some sleep himself.

Chapter Forty-Four

Clint and Reeves met out in front of the hotel the next morning, walked to the livery and collected their horses. In plain sight of the entire town, they rode down the main street and away. To all watching, it looked as if they were leaving town . . .

***

Lester Dent sat in a chair in front of the Last Race Saloon and watched as Clint Adams and Bass Reeves rode past him and out of town. When they were gone, he cackled, stood up and ran.

***

About a mile outside of town they reined in and turned.

"Did you see Dent in front of the saloon?"

"I did."

"Okay," Clint said, "that should convince people we left. Now we go back."

"We can't just ride back in," Reeves said.

"We'll stop a short distance outside of town, hide our horses, and walk into town to the doctor's office."

"And hopefully, go unseen."

"Yes."

"Okay," Reeves said, "it's your plan."

"Let's go," Clint said.

***

Dent knocked on the cabin door, which Butler opened. Behind him, White and Barry groaned and came awake.

"They left," Dent said. "They're gone."

"Adams, Reeves and Starr?" Butler asked.

Dent's face fell.

"Uh, no," he said. "Adams and Reeves rode out. Sam Starr must still be in the doctor's office."

"Then go back there and wait until Starr leaves, then let me know."

"And then I get my bottle?" Dent asked.

"Then you get your bottle."

Dent cackled, turned and ran back towards town.

"Whatta we do now?" Mike Barry asked.

Butler turned and said to the two men, "Wake the hell up!"

***

Clint and Bass Reeves managed to walk back to town and make it to the back of the doctor's office without being seen. Sam Starr had remembered to leave the door unlocked. As they entered and walked down the hall Clint called out, "Sam?"

"Here," Starr called back.

He was in the room with his wife. Clint and Reeves entered, and Belle Starr turned her head to look at them.

"Good-mornin'," she said.

"Good-morning, Belle," Clint said. "How are you feeling?"

"Much better," she said. "Sam told me your plan. I think I'm ready to be the bait."

"You won't have to do anything but lie there," Clint assured her. He looked at Starr. "Did the doc come by?"

"Not yet."

"Maybe we can get this done before he does," Clint said. "But nothing's going to happen until people see you leave town, as well. You better get going."

Sam Starr leaned over and kissed his wife.

"I'll be back," he said.

"I'll be here," she assured him.

Starr nodded to Clint and Reeves, and left.

"Now what?" Belle asked.

"Now we wait," Clint said.

Chapter Forty-Five

When the knock came at the cabin door the three men turned their heads. Butler walked to the door and opened it.

"He's gone," Dent said. "Sam Starr rode out a little while ago."

"Okay," Butler said, "let's get ready."

"What about my bottle?" Dent asked.

Butler shoved some money into his grubby hand and said, "Take two."

Dent ran back to town while Butler closed the door.

"Get your guns," he said. "We're goin' in."

"We?" Mike Barry asked.

"That's right," Butler said. "I'm gonna make sure it gets done, this time."

***

Clint looked out the front window without being seen.

"Anythin'?" Reeves asked.

"Not yet."

"Maybe we shoulda got somethin' to eat before we started this," Reeves said. "I'm starved."

Clint reached into his pocket, came out with a few pieces of beef jerky.

"Hey," Reeves said, accepting one. "Now we just need somethin' to drink."

"Hey!" Belle Start called from the other room.

Clint and Reeves went in. She pointed.

"I think the doc has some whiskey in that cabinet."

Reeves walked to it, opened the door and drew out a bottle of whiskey.

"I'll take some of that," Belle said, "and some jerky."

They found glasses and passed out three drinks and three pieces of jerky. Belle managed to get herself propped up on one elbow so she could eat and drink.

"That's better," she said. "I've been on my back for too long."

"If you're feeling better," Clint said, "maybe you can handle this."

He had taken his .32 Colt New Line out of his saddle-bags before they left their horses and tucked it into his belt. Now he passed it over to Belle.

"Hell, yeah," she said, accepting it. "Maybe if your plan works, I can help."

"You just relax," Clint said. "We're going to close that door, and once the shooting starts, if anybody comes through it, that's when you fire."

"Got it."

"Now all we've got to do is wait."

***

Butler led Ted White and Mike Barry down the street, then called them to a halt. There were people walking back-and-forth, doing what they normally did, unaware that this was not a normal day.

"We'll wait until there's not so many people on the street," Butler said. "Then White, I want you goin' in the back."

"Right."

"Mike, you and me are goin' in the front."

"Front door? What about that window?"

"Good idea," Butler said, "you take the door, I'll take the window."

"Why do I get the door?"

"Because you got the shoulders for it," Butler said. "Just smash it in and start shootin'."

Barry looked at the bony shoulders on Bart Butler and said, "yeah, okay."

***

After a couple of hours Belle also pointed out where Doc Hewitt had a coffee pot, so Clint put on a pot and they all had some.

"Good God, your coffee is strong," Reeves said. "We ain't out on the trail, you know."

"Trail coffee's the only coffee worth drinking," Clint said.

"Says you."

"I like it, too," Belle shouted from behind her closed door.

"See?" Clint said.

Reeves went to the window and looked out.

"Not many people on the street and it's almost mid-day," he said.

"Not too many storefronts in the area," Clint observed. "If they're going to hit us, it'll be when the street's deserted."

Reeves stepped away from the window.

"I wonder where the doc is?" he said.

"He probably decided to stay away until it's all over," Clint said. "Good decision, as far as I'm concerned."

"What if they don't come today," Reeves said, "or tomorrow? How long are you willin' to wait in here?"

"It's going to be today, Bass."

"How do you know?"

"The job wasn't done right the first time," Clint said. "They're going to take the first chance they have to get it done, and get out of town. That's today."

"I hope you're right," Reeves said. "By the time I get back to Fort smith. I may not have a job."

Chapter Forty-Six

"I changed my mind," Butler said.

"About what?" Mike Barry asked.

"Let's wait 'til dark," Butler said.

"What if Sam Starr comes back?" Ted White asked.

"If he rides up," Butler said, "we'll start by killin' him. Then we'll go inside and kill Belle."

"Why don't we just go in now and do it?" Barry asked.

"Because it's Belle Starr," Butler said. "If she's recoverin', then she's got a gun in there, and she knows how to use it."

"You're afraid of Belle Starr?" White asked.

"I ain't afraid of 'er," Butler said. "I'm just bein' . . . careful."

Ted White and Mike Barry exchanged a glance, then shrugged, Butler was calling the play, and he was paying.

***

Sam Starr went home, decided to have a drink or two to celebrate Belle's recovery, had one or two—or three—too many, and fell asleep.

He was out of the play.

J.R. Roberts

***

"Well, it looks like they're going to wait for dark," Clint said.

"I thought the doc would be lookin' in by now," Reeves said.

"He's probably waiting for it to be over."

"And I thought Starr'd be comin' in the back by now," Reeves added.

"He did some pretend drinking last night," Clint said.

"Are you thinkin' he did some real drinkin' today?" Reeves asked.

"Maybe he's celebrating Belle's recovery."

"It's a little lonely in here," Belle called from behind her closed door.

Clint opened the door.

"I thought we'd let you get some sleep."

"I'm bait," she said. "Bait don't sleep. Leave the door open so I can at least hear what you guys are saying."

"Bass was just wondering where Sam was," Clint admitted.

"If Sam went home and got drunk while I'm lying here as bait, I'm gonna make him pay," she said. "And if he's in a whorehouse—"

"He wouldn't do that," Clint said.

"He would and he does," she said.

"But not while you're shot."

"Ain't like he could come in here and poke me if he felt like it," she said.

"Look, he's worried about you," Clint said. "It'd make sense if he went home and had a few, not if he went to a whorehouse and did the same."

Clint turned to look at Reeves, who rolled his eyes. He'd known plenty of men who left their wives at home and went to whorehouses.

Clint decided it was time to turn the lamp up, since it was getting dark out.

***

Butler was about to send Ted White around to the back when he saw the light get brighter in the doctor's office.

"Hold on," he said.

"What now?" White asked.

"Come on, Butler," Mike Barry said, "we're ready."

"The light just got brighter inside," Butler said.

"So?" White asked.

"You think Belle Starr's well enough to get up, cross the room and turn the lamp up?"

"I think the doc left a lamp where she could reach it," Barry said. "Can we get this over with. Ted, go ahead."

White trotted across the street, and down the alley that led to the back of the doctor's office.

As Mike Barry started across the street, Butler figured he had no choice, and followed.

***

"Hear that?" Clint asked.

"I heard it," Reeves said.

"Heard what?" Belle asked.

"Board creakin'," Reeves said.

"Time to close the door," Clint said. "Remember, if I don't knock and the door opens, start shooting."

"Gotcha."

"You ready?" Clint asked.

"More than ready," Reeves said. They both kept their voices down. "I'll take the back."

Clint nodded, and Reeves crept down the back hall.

***

When the back door opened Reeves was ready. It could have been Sam Starr, or Doc Hewitt, but the fact that a gun appeared even before the man holding it was a dead giveaway.

"Drop it!" Reeves said.

Instead of dropping it the man holding the gun turned and started to bring the gun to bear on Reeves, who wasted no time pulling the trigger.

Just once . . .

***

Clint heard the single shot from the back, turned to face the front of the room. He could see the front door, and the window to the right, which was fortunate. As the door slammed open in response to one man's big, beefy shoulder, the glass of the window smashed and flew inward as another man broke it with his gun.

The beefy man stepped in, gun at the ready, while the man at the window stuck his gun into the room.

Clint drew and fired. He put two bullets in the beefy man's impossible to miss chest, then turned to the window and pulled the trigger a third time. He fired not at the gun sticking in the widow, or the arm and hand holding it, but at the bulk behind that. He heard a grunt as his bullet struck home and the gun disappeared.

Quickly, he stepped over the dead beefy man and through the door. He saw a man staggering away from the window, bleeding from the shoulder.

"Butler?" he said. "Don't—"

He wanted Butler alive to find out who had hired him, but the man wasn't having it. As he tried to bring his gun to bear, Clint had no choice but to fire again, putting the man down on his back.

"Clint!" Reeves shouted from inside.

"Here!" Clint answered.

Reeves came outside, stepping over the dead man, gun ready. He relaxed when he saw Clint standing there, unharmed.

"I got the one in the back."

"I got these two," Clint said. "The big one in the doorway's dead, but this one must be Butler. I'm hoping he's still with us."

"We'd better check" Reeves said.

They approached the fallen man cautiously in case he still had some fight left in him. But as they approached Clint saw the man's gun in the street, out of reach.

Clint leaned over him and felt for a pulse. There was none. He wasn't going to be able to tell Belle who had paid to have her shot, just that it was somebody in Detroit.

They heard running footsteps as townspeople began to locate the source of the shot and come to have a look.

"I better get inside with Belle," Clint said. "Just in case somebody else is sneaking in the back way."

"Go ahead," Reeves said. "This is the kind of scene I can handle."

Clint went inside, and was careful to knock on Belle's door so she didn't blow his head off when he went in.

***

The next morning Sam Starr still didn't show up, so Clint rented a buggy to take Belle Starr home in. He tied Eclipse to the back of it. He intended to leave the Oklahoma Territory directly from Belle and Sam's house. Bass Reeves had already departed for Fort Smith earlier that morning.

As they drove to her house Clint told her about Brad Butler and the telegram from Detroit.

"That's all we know," he concluded. "I'm sorry I can't tell you more, Belle."

"Never mind," she said. "You've helped me enough, just by keepin' me alive."

"I wish I could've kept you from getting shot in the first place," he said. "Roxy's going to have my ass for that."

"You tell Roxy to talk to me first," Belle said. She put her hand on his thigh. "I'm grateful to you for a lot of things."

As they pulled to a stop in front of the small, isolated cabin Clint asked, "Do you want me to go in with you?"

"No," she said, handing him his Colt New Line, "but you better take this back so I don't put a bullet in Sam's ass. I'm sure he's gonna be sleepin' one off."

"Take it easy on him," Clint said, as he helped her down, "He really was worried about you for days."

"Ah, I love 'im, I can't help it," she said, shaking her head. "But we're gonna fight. It's what we do." She reached up and kissed him. "When you see Roxy tell her I said thanks for sendin' you, and then you give 'er some of what you gave me the other night."

"Roxy and me, we're just friends," Clint said.

"Oh yeah," she said, with a smile, "she told me what good friends you are."

Historical Note

Later in life, after Sam Starr's death, Belle Starr was linked with several men bearing colorful names, such as Blue Duck, Jack Spaniard and Jim French. But eventually, in order to keep her house and property, she married a relative of Sam's named Jim July Starr. He was fifteen years younger than she was.

On February 3, 1889, while riding home from a dance, Belle stopped to drink at a neighbor's house, she was ambushed. The first shot knocked her from her horse. She was then shot a second time to make sure she was dead. Legend says she was shot with her own double-barreled shotgun. It was three days shy of her forty-first birthday.

There are several other versions of her death, but the murder had gone down in history as unsolved.

Coming September 27, 2019

THE GUNSMITH
451
The Last Way West

**For more information
click here:**

On Sale Now!

THE GUNSMITH
449

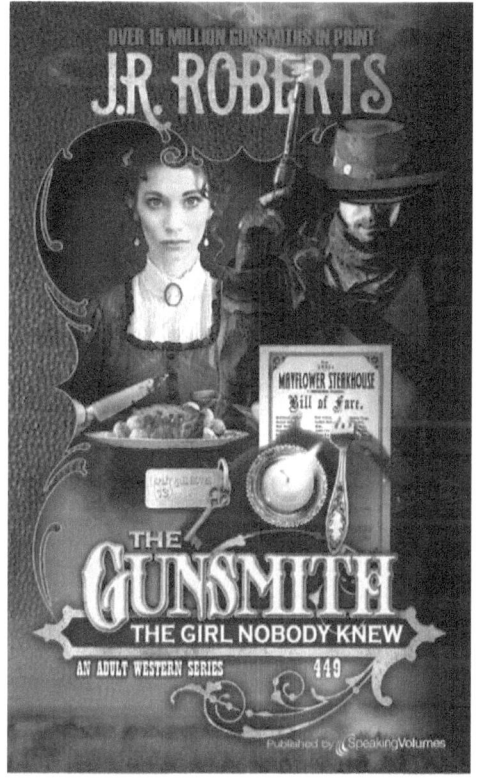

**For more information
visit:** www.SpeakingVolumes.us

On Sale Now!

THE GUNSMITH
448

For more information
visit:

On Sale Now!

THE GUNSMITH *series*
Books 430 – 447

**For more information
visit:** www.SpeakingVolumes.us

Coming October 15, 2019

Lady Gunsmith 7
Roxy Doyle and the James Boys

**For more information
click here:** www.SpeakingVolumes.us

On Sale Now!

Lady Gunsmith *series*
Books 1-6

**For more information
visit:**

On Sale Now!

TRACKER *series*
by Award-Winning Author
Robert J. Randisi (J.R. Roberts)

**For more information
visit:**

On Sale Now!

MOUNTAIN JACK PIKE *series*
by Award-Winning Author
Robert J. Randisi (J.R. Roberts)

For more information
visit:

50% Off
Audiobooks

www.ingramcontent.com/pod-product-compliance
Lightning Source LLC
Chambersburg PA
CBHW030447250626
47154CB00003BA/1172